ARIELLA'S
ESCAPE

BOOK ONE OF THE STARS AT ZENITH TRILOGY

CAROLEE CROFT

ISBN: 177504792X
ISBN-13: 978-1775047926

Cover Art by Kellie Dennis at Book Cover by Design
www.bookcoverbydesign.co.uk

CONTENTS

ACKNOWLEDGMENTS

A big thank you to Dallas Reagan and my writing and blogging friends Shehanne Moore, Christy Birmingham, Mike Steeden, and Zoolon. I never think of writing as a lonely job thanks to all your support.

Wild Nights – Wild Nights!
Were I with thee
Wild Nights should be
Our luxury!

- Emily Dickinson

Ariella's Escape

CHAPTER 1

Ariella had to admit, being an ambassador had its benefits. When she was shown into the chamber where she would be staying for the next three days, she had expected nothing but a restless night of practicing her arguments, only to find a gorgeous man lounging in her bed. She had heard rumors that the Chaldeans extended this sort of hospitality to their guests, and now here was definite proof of it, exemplified in the handsomest face she had ever seen – the body was draped with a light silken bedspread so not much of it was visible, but she could make out a broad set of shoulders. Blue eyes set beneath exquisite black brows examined her with curiosity. But then, evidently remembering his duty, the slave lowered his eyes in a gesture of humility.

"Greetings, Baroness of Leduryon" he pronounced, "I am here to entertain you this evening."

He spoke softly, and it was obvious he was someone who knew how to use his voice to persuade or seduce.

Ariella stood warily not far from the door while he reclined very much at ease in this chamber, surrounded by silken coverlets and pillows, on a bed raised on a platform and framed by two white marble columns. The slave threw the covers off, revealing a beautiful muscular body clothed only in something that looked like a silver loincloth. Ariella tried not to laugh at this attire but still a smile twitched at the corners of her lips.

She came forward, past the two columns and closer to the bed.

"Entertain me in what way?" she asked.

The man laughed, a remarkably free and unbridled sound that seemed surprising from a slave, if he was one.

"I'm sure being an ambassador is not easy," he said by way of an answer. "I would like to help you relax and feel at home."

"If there were handsome lads like you at home, I would have never left," she blurted out. This provoked another burst of his charming laugh.

She had to be careful, but something about him made her flirtatious.

"I can see why they made you a diplomat," he remarked.

Ariella sighed. She had never thought of herself as a diplomat, but Queen Esclairmonde was not to be refused, at least not if one didn't wish to see one's head on a pike. And the queen had decided that this mission required both subtlety and patience, combined with the visual display of a big sword.

At least when it came to the sword, Ariella knew she was perfect for the job.

Earlier that day, she had walked into the palace with her two-handed sword hung crosswise on her back and ten male guards walking in two perfect columns behind her. The courtiers seated on the marble steps all around the hall gaped, probably at her lack of grace. She knew she could compete with any rider and look the most poised on horseback, but walking, she felt too rough and ungainly for this sophisticated court.

The kingdom of Dezearre had long since kept the barbarians from overrunning the Northern Coast, and Ariella herself had taken part in a few skirmishes to repel them. However, to the Chaldeans, she may as well have been a barbarian herself.

The nobles strove to outshine each other with shimmering silks. Even the slaves who waited to attend upon their needs wore shiny garments in shades of gold and silver while Ariella sported a simple forest green tunic made of grey-eared rabbit wool, a light and comfortable fabric, cinched with a leather belt over brown hose. Although the tunic was not nearly as low-cut as the Chaldean ladies' dresses, she felt she could not be accused of appearing prudish because it was quite tight-fitting.

She noted the looks of many curious courtiers upon her, some examining her furtively from head to toe, but the only gaze that truly disturbed her was that of a young man who stepped forward to greet her in the throne room when she first arrived.

"Greetings, envoy of Queen Esclaimonde," he said. "I am Prince Theodos, and it is my pleasure to welcome you."

When he approached even closer, so close that his honey-scented breath wafted in her face, he said softly, so only she could hear, "You come here armed for warfare, trying to show Dezearre's strength. The ambitious young mountain wolf tests the leader's mettle by nipping at him. Well, you shall soon see, this old wolf is far from weak... Our empire was great once, and it shall be once again."

For a brief moment, she was lost for words. The prince, perhaps about the same age as her if she judged correctly, older than twenty but not yet thirty, with his beautiful ringlets of blonde hair had looked so sweet and innocent that this jab left her stunned.

"It is an honor to meet you, Your Highness," Ariella replied, speaking loudly enough for everyone assembled to hear. "In Dezearre, every man, woman, and child knows how to use at least one weapon should the Koroi threaten our lands again. My sword is with me everywhere I go, and it is not meant to show enmity."

That should teach him, and also remind everyone here that Dezearre had held its ground for many years without the empire's help. Not the most fortuitous beginning, but this was just the prince, she reminded herself. She would only have dealings with King Acheron.

The negotiations had not yet begun, would not until the next day, but Ariella was ready to assess her adversary. The king himself had no threatening words for her, thank the gods, and he smiled warmly when she approached and waved for her to stand when she touched down on one knee before the throne.

"Please forgive the ladies for staring," he said "Due to the nature of women's power here, which is concentrated on owning land rather than performing feats of arms, you appear exotic to them."

"I have heard women's power here is more subtle, but no less influential for it," Ariella replied.

"I'm afraid you're right," the king said, "for I do not recall one instance of making a decision on my own when my late wife was alive."

Ariella couldn't help but smile at his easy humour. King Acheron displayed none of the enmity that his son had shown. He spoke to her with the deepest respect, asked about her family and her estate, and according to the age-old custom, did not even remotely approach the subject of the coming negotiations. Maybe it was all an act, designed to lower her guard. The royal dinner that followed certainly did as much. The food was splendid, and Ariella barely restrained herself from gorging on the delicious pickor meat and quaffing the wines and cordials, knowing full well that tomorrow she would need all her mental faculties intact.

Wine was her weakness, and though she managed to control herself, even the one large goblet she drank was such heady stuff that its warmth snaked swiftly through her limbs, dangerous and sweet.

Now, seeing this handsome slave in her chamber she could not help but be wary. Was he sent here to learn her secrets, perhaps even to harm her? Poison had been used before as the means to eliminate several members of the royal family in Chaldea.

The young man seemed to have read her expression

correctly. He sprung from the bed and made a deep and reverent bow.

"Fear not," he declared, "For you are safe with me. My name is Demetrius, and I would never harm a lady I take to bed."

Now it was her turn to laugh. The combination of that loincloth with his lofty declaration was too much.

"You assume that is what will happen," she said coyly.

"If my lady wishes."

"And what do you wish?" she asked.

"I wish to please you," he replied, and his suggestive gaze seemed to confirm this desire.

Ariella walked past him and sat down on the bed, more out of weariness than anything else. The remarkably soft mattress invited her to sink into its embrace, but she was still somewhat guarded.

The slave Demetrius turned to her, a crooked smile on his lips. He was still studying her, probably trying to discern her mood.

"Do my looks not please you?" he asked, approaching the bed.

"On the contrary," Ariella admitted.

She wondered who had the honour of selecting the slave and how in the world beneath Epheor they had known he was just her type. He was a head taller than her, strongly built but not brutish looking. There was elegance in his muscular torso and his powerful arms. His face too had just enough masculine ruggedness balanced with a subtle refinement of features that made it heart-stoppingly beautiful.

It was strangely reassuring to know that he was not Chaldean, judging from his sun-bronzed skin, fine eyebrows and long brown hair, a shade so dark it was nearly black. And his eyes... like two pieces of a summer sky. She had always been a fool for a blue-eyed man. Judging by his elegant speech, very likely, he came from a noble lineage but was held here as a hostage to ensure peace with another kingdom.

"Then what is it, my lady?"

He sat down beside her on the bed, the scent of some innocent field flower with something more heady and musk-like tempting her to get closer to his bronzed body. She tried to discern his age... late twenties perhaps. His forehead was unlined, but there was something about him that made him appear older, a world-weariness perhaps behind his charming and carefree disposition.

There had been one or two times when she had bedded a man after less conversation than this, but this was strange territory with too many possible complications, and she could not afford to indulge herself on a whim. There was also his status to consider. As a slave, he was obviously not free in his choices, and she could sympathise with that. Ariella knew she would loathe being ordered to "entertain" guests in this manner were she in his place.

"Do my looks please you?" she asked tentatively.

"Yes," he replied, a slight hoarseness in his voice.

His eyes scorched her, and she had to look away.

"It's just that... I do not wish you to do this merely out of a sense of duty..." she said softly, "that is... if you did not want to..."

"My lady, I want to," he said. The certainty of his voice set a sudden flurry of fairy wings deep in her belly.

"I am flattered," she murmured. "But tell me, where are you from?"

He made himself more comfortable, half-facing her as they sat side by side on the bed.

"I'm the son of a poor baron of Sylcadia," he said with a careless shrug.

"How did you come to be here?"

"I was captured in battle... I was but fifteen at the time. An enemy lance unhorsed me, and by the time I managed to stand up in my considerable armor, I was surrounded on all sides by Chaldean blades placed at every single vital part of me. And I truly mean every single part. I thought it wise to surrender."

He smiled, and Ariella found herself smiling back. She could not help but like a man who viewed his own misfortunes with humor.

"And you have been here all this time, serving in the palace?" she inquired.

"Yes. Now, don't move."

He kneeled on the bed behind her. His hand reached for her shoulder, and she did not move away.

Why was she obeying him? She was a baroness of her own estate and obeyed no one. But his touch was so beguiling in its warmth, and she didn't want to move away from it. Now both his hands began to gently massage her upper back, her shoulders and neck. It felt divine. Taut and tangled muscles were quickly unwound and relaxed. She breathed deeper.

"Yes, thirteen years," the slave said, "But as you can see, I live in luxury. None of my duties are much more strenuous than this," he continued, caressing her arms with long strokes that revived her tired muscles. "And besides, being a stranger here, I am free of any truly demanding obligations such as those of kin and country."

That is very strange indeed, she thought, sooner to serve in a strange land than in your own... But she did not comment, for another thought suddenly struck her, that this was his way of coping with his enslavement, imagining that an even worse fate awaited him in his homeland. Perhaps, in a way he was right, for the duties of family were sometimes more binding than slavery.

Without another word, he reached underneath her knees and slid her fully onto the bed, lounging easily beside her. Again, she didn't object, didn't really have time to object, and his touch was so magnetic, this was even harder than denying herself the free-flowing royal wines. The pile of pillows at the head of the bed was so high that Ariella and her companion half-sat, reclining on the soft mound of silk.

"You must miss your home, I imagine," Demetrius said.

"Not at this exact moment," she admitted, darting a quick look at him. There was still so much fire in his expression, so she turned her gaze to the shiny swirling pattern of the bedcover. "But you know, I've been missing Jaquelle, my nursemaid. She's like a mother to me. And my hounds… they are such funny creatures."

"Funny? Not ferocious?" he queried.

"I rarely take them hunting," she admitted, adjusting her position among the pillows, "My late mother and father did, may the stars light them to their rest. The dogs are like companions and friends… especially Ric, the swifthound. He will steal food right off the table when he thinks I'm not paying attention and then looks very pleased with himself, his snout splattered with springberry sauce. Jaquelle thinks I spoil the dogs."

But Ariella had needed the laughter, the companionship of the dogs after the deaths of her parents. People talked too much and gave little comfort, while animals seemed to be able to bring comfort without saying anything.

"I am sorry to hear about your parents," he said softly.

"It was hard at first, but I am used to it," she smiled, reliving an old memory of when her parents were still alive, "My parents had tried to take me hunting, but my heart was never in it. It just doesn't seem sporting."

"I've always thought so too," he said, looking at her now with something more than just lustful interest, "I used to like simply riding through the forest in silence. My family thought I was mad…"

Ariella chuckled. She could not believe she was talking to him so easily, and yet she felt he was worth confiding in, that he was truly listening.

"Now tell me the truth, Demetrius," she asked, a smile playing at the edges of her lips, "Did the king send you here to find out my secrets?"

"The truth…" he lay back, cradling his head in his hands, a pose that the huge muscles of his chest stand out even more. "The truth is, this is a gesture of hospitality. But yes, he did want me to report anything you might say in regards to the negotiations. However, I don't believe that he was interested in any information regarding your swifthounds, so that secret is safe with me."

Ariella burst out laughing. She wanted to playfully slap his shoulder, but she was afraid of where it may lead.

"I knew it!" she exclaimed, "But does he really expect me to spill the muckpitts to you, especially when you've just told me of his plan?"

"I admit, I find it rather far-fetched myself," he replied, "but then again, when I'm embracing you in the heat of passion…" he scooped an arm under her and rolled her over to face him, "who knows what political secrets you might reveal."

When he had first seized her in mock abandon, she laughed, but then feeling the embrace of his strong arms around her, seeing his face just inches from her own, she suddenly froze, not wanting him to let go.

"It's doubtful I will reveal anything," she said slowly, "but we won't know until we try, will we?"

They lay there facing each other, and he still did not let go. This seemed so wrong, Ariella thought. She knew she was in danger here, and that this man could very well be posing as a friend to gain her trust, though she knew not for what purpose. The ease with which he confessed to being sent to her bedchamber as a spy was suspicious, or on the other hand it could mean that he was no spy at all, that he was only teasing her.

She couldn't read much in the clear blue fount of his eyes, more liquid than fire now, except a strong yearning for closeness.

His lips were slightly open, just inches away from hers. She realized she was now beyond any reasoning. She leaned into him, inhaling that ravishingly innocent smell, and her lips just lightly touched his.

Ariella suddenly wondered if she had had too much to drink after all, for in that moment when their lips had barely touched, she felt as if his lips were the most sensuous, delicious lips she had ever kissed.

As if disbelieving her own senses, she pulled back for a moment – though a moment long enough to see he looked as overwhelmed as she was – and then her lips encountered his once more, with a more determined pressure… Ariella was completely lost in the kiss, which sent the whole room spinning and the blood rushing through her body in a furious tempest.

His hands, which had been so calming just moments before, now aroused her as they roved over her back, her buttocks, her thighs. Those hands made her feel beautiful, flowing over all her curves and hollows, setting aflame everything they touched.

Breathless, she still could not stop kissing him. She pulled away briefly to remove her tunic. He watched, mesmerized, as she undressed most decisively. She sent her leather boots clattering to the floor and peeled off her hose. Her strong, lean body was all but revealed to him, all save her breasts, wrapped up in a cream colored length of fabric that criss-crossed over her shoulders.

She put the end of the strip in his hand, and his hand trembled with desire barely repressed.

"Shall I?" he asked.

Ariella nodded. He began to slowly unwind the fabric, savoring the sight of more and more of her skin revealed, one swathe at a time.

But she didn't give him much time to admire her breasts, driven by an urge to rub up against him, delighting in the touch of his naked skin against hers. His breathing quickened. His hands planed up and down her back with even more vigor, then squeezed her buttocks mercilessly. She gasped, feeling a stab of desire between her thighs.

She ached for him to fill her, and she reached for the silver loincloth. He helped her untie the straps that held it, letting it swoop to the floor. His manhood stood erect, its size impressive and slightly intimidating. It hardened even more when she grasped it, gently caressing its length. Her eyes held his as she touched him.

Perhaps other, more modest women would not have immediately grabbed the thing that they yearned for, but

Ariella was not one of them. She saw in his eyes the passion spark even brighter at her bold touch.

Ariella was still aware of the danger, but now she had come too far. Now, it only excited her more to think that she didn't know this man at all, and that she was about to throw herself into the torrent of both their desires.

Before she could stop herself, her lips closed round him and she explored him with her tongue. He lay back, surrendering to her onslaught, breathing raggedly and uttering soft groans.

The sound of his voice increased the passionate longing in her belly. She moved up face to face with him and found his gaze again. He was more than ready. She knew his duty must be to do whatever she needed for her pleasure, and although she could also see that currently he didn't seem too unhappy, still she wished she could tell him that he was free to do what he wanted, but somehow she could not find the words. How could she, when no reasonable thoughts or words could be formed, with his touch more potent than any wine?

When her hips descended, finding his hardness, it felt so incredibly big and taut. She uttered a small gasp as what felt tender at first began to send waves of pleasure surging through her lower body.

He was breathing heavily, completely enthralled by her, but he did not rush her. He let her become more comfortable with his considerable size as she found a slow, grinding rhythm. Very soon, her hips began to move faster, each thrust enflaming her more and more. She was riding him fast and hard. The huge monolith of his torso rocked beneath her, his hips responding to her thrusts.

"By the living stars, you are beautiful," he breathed.

But soon they were both beyond words. All she could sense was the sweetness of his scent and the wild rhythm of her own body, instinctively moving with a fierce and relentless pace. She leaned forward, letting her hair tickle his chest.

She leaned ever closer, until she was able to kiss his lips and bury her face in his dark locks, and brush her cheek against his.

Her rapture mounted until her body felt flooded to the brink.

Oh, she never wanted it to end… but finally it ebbed, and when it did, she felt a sweet release as if a gentle wave had washed her up onto a soft, sandy shore.

She still didn't have the words to say to him. She wanted him to be free with her, but for that, they would have to wait for the next night. The usually voluble slave was quiet too. He only kissed her lips with a gentleness that soothed her. Only three nights here… they would make good use of that time, she thought as she fell asleep.

CHAPTER 2

The rising sun gilded the strange, luxurious guest room that was hers for these few days, as if there was not enough golden opulence here. And next to her lay the slave who resembled a bronze god, and who had pleasured her so eagerly the night before.

She tried to memorize his features. His long black lashes cast pointed shadows on his cheeks. His skin was unbelievably smooth, with just a hint of stubble giving him a slightly more natural look than that demanded of a well-groomed servant.

She could not imagine that he truly did not want to escape this life. There was definitely more to his story that he wasn't telling.

He must have felt the intensity of her gaze because his eyelids slowly lifted to reveal those stunning sky-blue eyes she admired.

Ariella felt slightly embarrassed at being thus caught staring, but it was too late to look away. Doing so would have caused further embarrassment, so she smiled at him instead, and he returned the smile.

Ariella believed she could be subtle at times. But not this time.

"Will you be here again tonight?" she asked.

He freed his hand from the covers to stroke her shoulder.

"Of course, if you wish it... Ariella."

He no longer called her "my lady," and she liked that.

Someone knocked softly on the door, so softly that Ariella at first thought it might be coming from the next room.

She quickly found her tunic and pulled it on. She sat herself on the side of the bed in what she hoped was a graceful pose.

"Enter?" she called out uncertainly.

The door opened slowly to reveal a slave girl dressed in the palace's usual dazzling style. Her silver undergarments barely covering her breasts and loins were of the same material as Demetrius', and over these she wore a long, semi-transparent robe that shimmered with golden radiance in the morning sunlight. In her hands she held a small case of tawny leather.

"Good morning, my lady," the girl pronounced in a hushed voice, "I am at your service. If you will permit me, I will help prepare you for the day... not that your beauty needs any additions, but perhaps a few touches of color to enhance your natural radiance?"

"No, do not trouble yourself." Ariella smiled politely, feeling a slow blush creep into her cheeks. She noted wryly to herself that she had probably not blushed at all at the idea of being entertained by a sex slave, but for some reason this was altogether too much.

Her barony was not one of the richest, and she never had servants attend upon her beauty needs. All she ever did was brush out her own hair and plait it or tie it back with a leather thong. She had never worn powder or any other adornments, and to have another woman apply them to her face would feel beyond strange.

The slave girl bowed, but would not retreat. Her large eyelids, painted a shimmering blue shade, were lowered out of fear or respect.

"Please, my lady," she murmured, "It would be an honor for me. And His Majesty may be offended if you refused this courtesy."

Ariella rolled her eyes, muttering, "I wonder how would he

like to be painted?"

The female slave looked close to tears. Her face struggled not to contort itself into a grimace.

"Please, my lady. I will be punished if my duty is not done."

Demetrius sat up in the nest of pillows, looking intently at the girl.

"Ciara," he addressed her, "The king does not usually insist on such ceremony. Did he truly say he would punish you if you did not complete the task? Or was it the Master of Rituals?"

"It was the king," she replied, her eyes still lowered.

Ariella sighed. She supposed every diplomat had to deal with such inconveniences.

"Very well then. Just make it as quick as you possibly can."

Ciara approached the bed hesitantly. She reached into her leather case and removed a small brush. Then she dabbed the brush into a glass jar that held a fiery red, viscous cream.

The slave inclined her head to one side, judging the best place to begin the application. Ariella sat still and looked straight ahead. She began to feel very awkward as the brush approached her lips.

Just as it was a mere inch away from her face, Demetrius hurtled past her, grabbing Ciara's wrist and tackling the girl to the floor.

"Demetrius, what–" Ariella exclaimed, but suddenly stopped herself. A horrible suspicion suddenly sent a chill up her spine, and she realized that Demetrius action made perfect sense.

Meanwhile the slave girl struggled fruitlessly, attempting to escape Demetrius grasp. He snatched the brush from her tiny hand and then released her, leaving her in a sobbing heap on the floor.

He stood up and brought the sticky, red bristles of the brush very slowly up to his face, sniffing them.

"Carrion berry," he pronounced.

"What is it?" Ariella asked.

"It grows in the bog lands of the north, and it's a deadly poison. It will stop your heart in three minutes, but not before making you wish it were sooner."

"No, it's not true. I had no evil intentions," the girl protested.

"Then maybe you wouldn't mind?" Demetrius asked, pointing the brush at her.

At once, she sprang up and retreated several paces away from him. Her teary eyes were fixed upon the brush with horror. Her lips quivered.

Demetrius looked unrelenting. He had bounded from the bed perfectly nude, and his muscular form now suggested not only pleasure but also violence. Ariella could scarcely believe that her jovial companion of the night could now be so menacing. More importantly, she could now believe that he had saved her from a horrible death.

"King Acheron didn't send you, did he?" Demetrius approached the girl, seizing her and threatening her with the brush as if it were a dagger.

She shook her head.

"What is this? Why is this happening?" Demetrius seemed to grow more and more agitated. "Tell me now or by all the besotted stars I will–."

"Did you not hear the screaming in the night?" the girl whispered, "King Acheron is dead. Prince Theodos now rules the land."

Demetrius released her, and she collapsed to the floor.

"The prince had his father killed?" he asked in a lifeless voice, staring blankly.

The girl nodded.

"And he sent you to kill Lady Ariella," he stated in that same flat tone.

The girl nodded again and recommenced sobbing. Demetrius bit his lips, probably feeling guilty for his part in reducing her to this state. Or at least, Ariella hoped he felt some remorse. She did not want to think of him as being completely ruthless.

"I am done for…" Demetrius whispered. "Unless… Ciara, I know he must have threatened you into doing this, and I'm sorry I did the same. But do not fear. You can escape the palace. Come with me."

"No," Ciara sobbed. "It is too late. We are all under his command now."

"I refuse," Demetrius objected, "Better to die trying to escape than to live under his rule. You can come with me, and I will do my best to protect you."

The girl only shook her head.

Demetrius hastened to find his discarded clothing, refitting himself with his silver loincloth, a blue silk robe, and a pair of golden sandals.

"Are you coming?" he asked Ariella.

"Where?" she wondered.

She was more than a little stunned.

"Away from here, obviously. If we escape together, we may have a chance."

"But my mission…" she began.

"The man now in power wants you dead. I think it's safe to say this mission did not go all that well."

"Oh gods, you're right," she said.

Ariella had been too dumbfounded to act. In her short and relatively simple life, she had never experienced treachery on such a grand scale. Now, she quickly sprang for the rest of her clothing and tried not to let her hands shake as she pulled on her boots.

In her scramble to dress, she suddenly realized that she had failed to notice Ciara slipping out the door as quietly as she had come.

"Ever-blasted stars," Demetrius growled when he too realized Ciara was gone. "We must depart. Now."

Ariella snatched the scabbard that contained her sword and hung it across one shoulder, the sword resting slantwise against her back.

They were heading for the door when six palace guards burst into the room. Arrayed in the finest chain mail vests worn over red uniform jackets, they were armed with halberds and short daggers that hung from their belts in case of closer combat.

There were six of them, and they were all tall, burly men. Unarmed as he was, Demetrius stepped forward to face them.

"It's over for you, covetous dog," the guard spat. "The king who favored you is dead, and soon you'll be giving him my regards in the afterlife."

Demetrius fixed him with an icy stare.

"Was it you who killed the king, Bran?" he asked.

The guard laughed unpleasantly. "Wouldn't you like to know? But I'm not here to answer your questions. Kill the woman! Take the dog of a slave alive!" he commanded his men.

But it was Ariella who began the fight. A throwing knife she had hidden in her cloak now served her well as it whooshed across the room and embedded itself in the throat of the guard who stood beside the leader. He opened his mouth but remained mute with shock, and two of his comrades caught him as he collapsed. His sword fell from his hand, but before it even touched the ground, Demetrius leaped towards it, caught its hilt, and rolled across the floor to rise up in a defensive stance.

Two of the guards were on him instantly, while the leader and two others charged Ariella. She made a show of charging towards them too, but in the last second, she stepped behind a column, letting it stop the momentum of two of the guards, while her two-handed blade blocked the leader's halberd and pushed it back.

She heard a bloodcurdling scream from the other side of the room, but didn't have the time to see whether Demetrius or a guard was hurt. One of her attackers did get distracted by it, and Ariella lunged at him. His light chain mail was no match for the full force of the two-handed blade. It sliced through his collar bone and halfway down his chest.

More horrible screams filled the splendid chamber.

At the same time, her other two opponents swung their halberds – she saw them from the corner of her eye. With a downward motion of her wrists, she extracted the sword from the guard's dying body, and she dove to the floor, the two halberds just missing her and colliding with each other instead.

Immediately, she had to roll away, for the relentless halberds pursued her. They struck, embedding themselves in the wooden floor, and this bought her a second of time to rise and assume a fighting stance.

Out of the corner of her eye, she saw Demetrius approach. He lunged for one of her opponents, while the other one suddenly turned and fled.

Ariella realized in that instant that none of the guards must leave the room. The last thing they needed was the entire army after them. If the prince was waiting for his guards to bring back her dead body, he would have to wait in uncertainty a little longer, buying them some time.

Luckily she had another knife, which flew relentless as fate. The blade lodged itself in the fleeing man's thigh, and he stumbled. Despite the pain, he hobbled towards the door, knowing it was his only chance, but Ariella now caught up with him, running him through with her blade without even giving him the chance to turn around.

"I'm in no mood to be chivalrous," she murmured as the guard collapsed, his hands still seeking the door to salvation.

She turned to witness Demetrius throw the last remaining guard to the ground and stab him in the heart with ruthless efficiency. The guard screamed once as he was run through, and once more as the blade was quickly removed from his chest. He was still alive, uttering only faint moans.

"They deserve no mercy," Demetrius assured her, seeing her troubled expression, "They have betrayed their king. This must have been months in the planning…"

No longer a palace slave, despite his attire, a ruthless warrior stood before her.

"You're right," she conceded.

Though she had fought in a few skirmishes, she had never experienced such violence in what would otherwise be a comforting and homely setting. The shock must have been still evident on her face.

"We'll go by way of the servants' quarters," Demetrius said, "Come!"

"My guards!" she exclaimed. "Do you think they'll be marked for death too?"

He nodded grimly. "Most likely."

"I would like to save them if I can. They could come with us. As you said, there is strength in numbers, and together we may have a chance of fighting our way free."

"How many are there? Ten?"

"Yes," she replied.

"That is too many. The two of us could more easily slip away unnoticed. But ten…"

"Oh, what does it matter?" Ariella exclaimed, "I can't just leave them to die."

"They're probably dead already. We don't have time for this."

"Yes we do. They are just quartered in that room on the far side of the hallway…"

"Then let us be swift," Demetrius said.

He looked out into the hallway and saw that it was deserted. Ariella followed him, and together they walked swiftly, feeling completely exposed until they reached the room.

Ariella could barely suppress a scream of horror and frustration. The ten men who made up her guard were now but corpses. They lay about the room, beautiful silver drinking goblets fallen beside them. Perhaps the same slave who had failed with the rouge had succeeded here.

These were the queen's guards, not her own, and she had not really known them very well. They had kept her at a respectful distance, but she had learned a little about them on the journey.

"You will be avenged," she said softly to her fallen guards. "Sleep well."

Turning to Demetrius, she then asked, "Can you get us to the stables? I can't leave without my horse."

"By the living stars, are you mad? Are lives are in danger

every moment we stay here."

"And will be for as long as we remain on Chaldean soil. It is my understanding that horses could get us away more swiftly."

"They will also allow us to be tracked more easily..." he grumbled, "But you may have a point. To the stables, then."

He led her down the twisting corridor. At each turn, they stopped and peered around the corner, but no guards barred their way. The castle's inhabitants did not leave their rooms either. A terrified silence reigned everywhere among the echoing halls. Ariella wanted to say or at least whisper something to dispel it, but she could think of nothing.

They entered the servants' quarters through an unobtrusive door at the end of the hallway.

Here, slaves and servants slept on pallets in small niches. The two fugitives passed an endless row of these. Some of the slaves were already rising and washing up using small basins or dressing themselves according to their duties, some in glamorous silver and gold silk, others more plainly in white, black, or grey linen robes.

The two fugitives turned round a corner and encountered a series of doors. Demetrius took a key from his robe and opened one of the doors onto a tiny but fairly opulent room. It was beautifully decorated with pictures of trees and animals.

"My quarters," he explained, though Ariella had already guessed it.

He found some sort of package in the back of a drawer and stuffed it into a pocket of his robe. He tied the sword he had taken from slain guard to his waist and tucked it inside his clothing. Then he removed a grey servant's robe and a grey hood from the drawer and passed them to Ariella.

"Put these on. You will not stand out as much, and hopefully we can leave here without pursuit."

Ariella did so, unbuckling her sword. The floor-length robe covered her foreign-looking tunic, while the hood, which had a small cape attached at the shoulders, completely concealed her chestnut hair and shaded most of her face. She tried to tuck the sword and its belt unobtrusively under her arm.

Then Demetrius took one more glance around the tiny room and ushered Ariella out. He didn't bother to close the door as they left.

"I don't need any of the trinkets I've gained during my life here," he explained, "but I thought a little food and spending money would not go amiss."

Ariella realized that he must have been keeping that package and that robe while planning his own escape.

They hurried down a flight of steps and onto the ground floor of the castle. They ended up in another warren of servants' niches and bedchambers, and Demetrius led the way decisively until they finally stood in a doorway that led outside.

People milled about in the courtyard. Kitchen servants fetched vegetables, children played, and a few guards lounged by a small gate that led to out of the castle and into the city. The gate was open, and it seemed people passed through unhindered.

"Now," Demetrius said, "let us walk to the stables."

They passed among the usual servants, unnoticed, and entered the darkness of the stables. Ariella was comforted by the smell of hay and horses. She quickly made her way to a white leopard-spotted horse that nickered in greeting.

"Shh! Quiet, Destiny. We can't make a big scene of our departure. Understand?"

The horse snorted softly, and she hoped he understood. He was nervous and unreliable, like most horses, but at least his speed and strength would be a benefit if they were to get clear the palace.

"We don't have time to saddle him," Demetrius whispered.

"Agreed. Can you ride bareback?"

"Of course. But it will look less suspicious if we are not seen leaving together. You lead the horse and I will walk a few paces behind you as if I am just going into town for my own business. Remember, you're a servant. If anyone asks, the horse needs a new shoe, and you're taking it to the blacksmith."

Ariella nodded. There were people from all corners of the old empire here, and even if she had to speak, her Dezearre dialect wouldn't be anything unusual.

Destiny wore a simple bridle with a rope attached to it, and she used this to lead him out of the stable.

She emerged into the sunlit courtyard, blinking in the brightness. The guards at the postern gate still lounged in carefree attitudes, and she doubted they would stop and question her since they didn't do so for any of the multitude of people coming and going. Confidently, she led the horse onwards. She didn't look anyone in the eye, focusing her gaze just above the horizon, where numerous buildings beckoned her beyond the gate.

The guards did not single her out.

She walked on until she was past the gate, her heart hammering. Here, she mounted the horse and prepared to ride off. Demetrius was almost through the gate. He nodded to the guards who obviously knew him and gave him a nonchalant greeting.

She rode on, not wanting to show too much interest, but a great clanging of armor and stomping of feet made her turn back to look. It came not from the guards at the gate but from somewhere in the courtyard.

A dozen guards bullied their way forward, led by Prince Theodos himself. In another instant, the prince spotted Demetrius.

"There he is!" the prince cried. "Take him alive."

Theodos had long blonde curls and a boyishly pretty face. But at this moment, just like when she first met him, a note of cruelty belied his innocent features.

The guards advanced, but Demetrius had to take only a few steps before he was out of the gate. Ariella squeezed the rope in her hands, while Destiny pranced, sensing her impatience.

Yet something made Demetrius hesitate.

"Come on," Ariella whispered.

But he did not move. Then, without warning, he charged at the prince.

Ariella could not believe what she was seeing. Instead of taking the final few steps to freedom which lay beyond the gate, Demetrius attacked Prince Theodos.

"I knew you wouldn't miss this chance," the prince said smugly, deflecting his thrusts.

Demetrius fought with the fury of a madman, but the prince did not retreat. He parried every slash and gave no ground. Ariella marvelled at his skill in spite of herself. The guards tried to circle around to Demetrius' back so as to capture him more easily, but he saw this and continued to shift his position.

"Demetrius!" she called.

But he either did not hear or did not wish to escape.

Well, this did not concern her. Ariella turned the horse away from the castle, squeezing his flanks to urge him forward. Destiny began to trot. She was going to escape Chaldea with her life, something she had not thought entirely possible just minutes ago.

Then why did she feel so uneasy?

Then she cursed, and guided the horse with a simple pressure of her right knee back to the castle gate.

She charged through the open gate, making for the clump of guards who now surrounded Demetrius. One of them went for Demetrius' legs, making him lose his balance and fall to the ground. Two other guards tried to pin him down, but he threw them off with the explosive strength of his fury.

At this moment, Ariella rushed into their midst, and the three guards closest to Demetrius were all knocked out of the way easily by the horse's huge bulk. Two other guards pushed aside, Demetrius regained his footing. Ariella offered her arm, he clasped it and was up on the steed behind her.

Now they charged through the courtyard towards the closing gate, but they were too late. The guards had drawn it shut, and Ariella turned Destiny sharply about, pursued by the same guards who had so recently let her pass through.

She looked for a way out, but there was none, save for a narrow staircase that led up to the battlements. It was this path that she chose.

"My horse will help us escape," she said to Demetrius without turning as she looked up towards their goal and willed the horse to climb, "Trust him."

Demetrius did not have time to reply, for he was just slashing at a guard who pursued them. The guard evaded the sword but tripped and tumbled down the stairs.

Another sentry who came running along the parapet and met them as they reached the top landing lashed out at Destiny with his sword, but was knocked several feet away by his hooves.

Now, for a few split seconds the parapet was theirs; the other guards led by the prince had not yet caught up.

"How is your horse supposed to save us now?" Demetrius asked, glancing at the approaching guards.

The wall was at least thirty feet tall, and the only way to descend would be to fall to their deaths or try to take back the narrow stairway which was already swarming with guards.

"No time to explain," Ariella replied.

She drew a red crystal from a pocket of her cloak and without wasting another moment she swerved the horse into the recess between two teeth of the battlement. For a moment the horse and riders seemed suspended in the recess, the horse's forelegs hovering over thin air but then Destiny took the leap off the castle wall.

Ariella threw the red crystal into the air before them, and it split apart into myriad crimson dust motes, forming a descending arc along which the horse could gallop down to the ground. Demetrius looked around him in bewilderment, but then shouted with triumph.

The horse looked by turns frightened, judging by the whites of his eyes showing as he goggled at the ground beneath him, and proud of himself.

The city's residents pointed and shouted. Houses streaked by.

Ariella turned back to see the rapidly increasing distance between her and the castle wall. Demetrius looked back too, just in time to see the prince arrive at the battlement from which they'd jumped. From here, he was nothing but a quickly diminishing figure. Below the riders, the closely pressed houses of the city flashed by. A few children pointed and shouted with glee, but they too were soon whisked away by Destiny's speed. At last, the red crystal path descended, and Destiny's hooves pounded on solid ground.

They landed at the edge of the city and galloped onwards along the brick-paved road. The crystal bridge behind them began to fall apart, its tiny pieces following the riders like a swarm of red bees. Suddenly, they coalesced into a flaming sphere and regained their shape as a crimson stone, landing in Ariella's hand. Without stopping the horse, she caught the talisman, and they rode on, leaving a high trail of dust behind them.

CHAPTER 3

Demetrius was stunned beyond words to see the warrior maiden use the ancient magic known only to Zaliati Warriors as easily as one would crack open a muckpitt. A mix of jealousy and admiration now crowned all the rest of his confusing feelings for her. He had always wished he could be a Zaliati, an invincible warrior like ones in the old legends. Instead he had spent the prime years of his life as a palace slave.

And he did not feel completely free, not as long as they remained in Chaldea.

Ariella slowed the horse to a trot and then a walk to allow it to rest after its mad sprint.

"Do you think they will try to capture us?" she asked.

"I have no doubt," Demetrius replied grimly.

On either side of the road lay open fields where crops ripened in the late summer sun. The two fugitives rode on, and Demetrius hoped they would not be seen by too many passing peasants. It was a hope that dwindled as he realized that they made quite a striking sight that attracted many a gaze: a handsome couple dressed like servants, riding a white, leopard-spotted horse that was fit for a baroness, or even a queen.

"I wish your horse were not the most recognizable animal

in the kingdom," Demetrius muttered.

"Well, it cannot be helped," Ariella replied irritably, "At least not for now. I may be able to disguise him once we are out of the view of the general populace."

"We shall be clear of the farms soon."

"What then?" she asked.

"Well… I trusted your horse, now will you trust me to guide us through the wilderness?"

"You didn't have much choice but to trust my horse," Ariella smirked, "but I'm finding it difficult to trust you."

"Why?" he asked, though he feared he knew the answer.

"I thought for a moment you had changed your mind and didn't wish to escape," she said. "Were you seeking your death in that courtyard?"

"You didn't have to return for me," Demetrius murmured, "Thank you."

Ariella shrugged. "I owed you my life. After all, you saved me from a deadly poison. The least I could do was to repay you. But why did you not escape at that moment? The gate was yet open. You could have made a run for it."

He hesitated with his answer. If only she knew the torture Theodos had inflicted on him, body and mind, she would not be asking. But he did not want her to know. At the same time, he understood that his actions must have seemed those of a madman.

"It was a good opportunity to kill Prince Theodos," he replied simply, "I want him dead. In that moment, I suddenly stopped thinking clearly. I truly didn't expect you to ride into that courtyard and rescue me."

She twisted around to look at him, making him suddenly breathless with desire at the reminder of how pliable her body could be. He felt the probing force of her gaze, knew she had many more questions, but she did not say anything. He had not been acquainted with her very long, but somehow he felt certain she was not a relentless person; there was something very noble about her. She would understand his desire for secrecy on this matter and respect it enough not to pry.

"Well," she said at length, "You led me out of the palace. And this country must be well known to you too."

"Unfortunately, yes," Demetrius said grimly. "I have been through this forest many a time, accompanying the king. We can head east until we reach the border of Dezearre. I shall see you safely to your kingdom, and then I will go on to Sylcadia."

"But there is no need for you to accompany me if it lengthens your journey to your kingdom," she said, perplexed.

"I have waited thirteen years to see Sylcadia again," Demetrius said, "but I can wait a little longer. You saved my life back in that courtyard, and I owe you a debt. I will see you home."

"It does seem wiser to travel together," she said at length. "There may be pursuit, or other dangers."

Even when talking of danger, she tended to speak in careless tones, as if she was always a little bit drunk.

She fell silent, while Demetrius felt a compulsive yet inexplicable desire to keep her talking because the sound of her voice was so seductive. If it had a visible color, her voice would be the color of the night sky, dark and deep, shimmering with stars. It sparked an unquenchable desire.

He wondered if part of the reason she agreed to let him accompany her was because she felt an attraction to him and wanted him to continue serving as her bed mate. It seemed too soon to bring up that subject.

A cart trundled by, driven by a middle-aged peasant who gaped at the sight of them.

Demetrius felt an odd sensation of pride that he was riding with such a beautiful lady. His hands held lightly to her waist, and he recalled holding all of her the previous night.

It was early evening when they passed the main cluster of farms; forested hillsides appeared to the east, and it was there that Demetrius guided the horse. They left the main road and headed into the woods.

Demetrius wondered what thoughts occupied his companion. He doubted she was still dwelling on the mystery of his hatred for Prince Theodos. No doubt she had her own concerns.

"Let us dismount," she suggested, "for Destiny must be weary."

Demetrius nodded, and they proceeded on foot as he led the way.

The sun was beginning to sink somewhere beyond the western hills, but it still shone brightly, piercing the foliage here and there with visible shafts of luminescence. Insects buzzed, assaulting both the horse and the humans. Destiny whipped his tail in all directions, while Demetrius and Ariella swiped fiercely every now and then at their own faces.

"Do you not think Prince Theodos would expect us to go this way?" she suddenly asked.

Demetrius stopped for a moment and turned to look at her. "He may."

She turned to face him, and he felt thoroughly tantalized and probed by that intense gaze once again. "Do you want him to catch up to us?" she demanded. "So you can try to kill him again?"

He shook his head. "You still don't trust me. What happened at the palace was a momentary lapse of judgment. I would never repeat that performance. Please believe me: I am only taking this route because it is the shortest, and because we're less likely to encounter people here. We risk pursuit no matter which direction we turn, but here in the forest we may be able to confuse our pursuers."

In the distance, he heard the whisper of a nearby stream.

"This way," he said, "the water will hide our tracks."

Ariella sighed. "I suppose I have no choice. I don't know these lands."

The music of the stream and its mossy smell were pleasant in this wooded wilderness. It was a broad and gentle stream, not too deep, so that it barely reached the horse's knees when they waded into the midst of it.

Demetrius gathered some water in his hands and spilled it over his face. It felt so good that he just dipped his whole head in.

He had not intended it to be anything but a cooling balm, but the water seeped down his chest, wetting his robe, which had not covered much of his chest to begin with. He felt her hunger before he saw it; the way she looked at him, then sharply turned away. There was no question about it, her desire was strong. She had been hiding it well until now.

"I wager you never thought to find yourself here at this time of the evening," Demetrius remarked, trying to mask his own lust.

He walked on again at a leisurely pace, and she followed suit, just a little ahead of him.

She smiled, glancing back. "At this exact time I would be discussing how many heads of cattle Queen Esclairmonde would give in exchange for some useless piece of arid, mountain land."

"Not useless," he remarked.

"What do you mean?" Ariella asked.

"You don't know? That land includes the Shadowed Summit, the realm of the Alchemist."

"I have heard the legends, but what is the use of the Alchemist if he even exists?"

"The Alchemist holds the key to restoring the empire. I am surprised the queen sent you here without any knowledge of the power that could be obtained from those mysteries."

"I thought my task was to assert our independence from Chaldea," she said, "Queen Esclairmonde told me that repeatedly. She said the land was just a token."

"That seems suspicious," Demetrius noted.

"It does now." she agreed.

"Prince Theodos wants that land. It is the only explanation for the timing of his overthrow of his father."

Ariella stopped walking, and the horse did too, snorting impatiently.

"You mean this was all to do with that godforsaken mountain?"

"I believe so," said Demetrius. "If Prince Theo tried to kill you, it means he does not care whether there is peace or war between your kingdoms. Killing you would have been the gauntlet thrown in the face of Queen Esclairmonde. Unless, the queen sent you here knowingly to your death. You didn't suspect anything?"

"You must think I'm a complete fool!" Ariella exclaimed.

"I think you were betrayed," he said.

"And therefore a fool," she concluded.

She splashed on through the water, and Demetrius followed a few paces behind. He cursed himself for bringing up this subject at all, when they could have been talking about their sleeping arrangements.

At length she said, without turning around, "And you may be right."

At nightfall, they stopped and made a small fire.

Demetrius was busy fanning the flames and adding more sticks, but out of the corner of his eye he saw his companion remove something from her pocket, the crystal, he guessed.

She stroked Destiny's neck, her hands gentle and beguiling. Then the crystal began to break apart as she worked the magic, sprinkling its dust from the horse's nose to its tail. Destiny's leopard spots began to fade, and in just a few moments his coat turned pure black. He shook his neck from side to side disdainfully.

"I know, you like your spots, but this should wear off after a few days. Patience!" Ariella said to her mount.

The horse merely snorted.

The pieces of the crystal slowly floated back into Ariella's hand, and when it was re-formed it looked dull and sparkless.

"That was the last of the power left in the crystal," Ariella said, looking at Demetrius across the fire. "It will need several days to be restored. Next time there's trouble, we'll have to improvise."

She sat down beside him.

"I'm sorry about earlier," she said, "I know you were trying to help me. Does he really believe there is something of worth there, I mean Prince Theodos?"

"I believe so, and he must as well. He's obsessed with

restoring the old empire."

"I noticed. But those are just old legends."

Demetrius couldn't believe she had so little interest. He pointed to the stars above them in the blackness of the sky, spotted with the forest's leafy canopy.

"Some people believe that the Spheres of Epheor the sky move with purpose, that the stars are gods looking down on us, others believe they're merely the fires of lifeless realms. What do you believe?"

She frowned slightly, her gaze fixed on the fire. "I believe in the gods, but I think they're cruel."

Demetrius didn't agree, despite everything he had endured. There had always been such a strong hope in his heart for freedom, and he had finally found it. But he did not want to pry, just as she had not pried into his secrets.

However, he hated the thought of such a young woman, so kind and noble, believing that life was essentially misfortune.

"There are so many stars in the sky," he said, "When I was captured, I had little chance of seeing my home ever again. At first, the hopelessness of my situation nearly destroyed me. But then I decided that among the thousands of stars, thousands of gods, there must be at least one that would shine its light on me... Maybe you are my lucky star."

Slowly, the corners of her lips lifted into the tiniest of smiles.

"I thought you said home was worse than slavery," she remarked teasingly.

"And I meant it," he replied, "My mother will put me to work the very same day I return, if not the very same minute, you can bet your last Ral."

They ate a small meal of dried meat, which had been concealed in Demetrius' escape package, as well as a few muckpitts they had picked on the marshy shore of the stream. The nutty taste of the muckpitts added a comforting touch of luxury to the otherwise simple meal. They cracked the outer shells of the fruits with the pommel of Ariella's sword. Now that he had a good look at it, Demetrius was amazed by the craftsmanship of the weapon. The cross guard had the shape of an eagle's wings, curving slightly outward, their tips pointing towards the enemy. The blade was not made of steel, but of some other metal that had a slight golden sheen, though it was obviously too light to be gold.

"Does your sword have a name?" Demetrius asked.

She shrugged.

"Why should every noble no matter how grand or small name their sword? It's so pompous. It's just a weapon, it does a job. That's good enough for me."

"The Nameless Sword then," he suggested.

Ariella made an act of gagging. "Even more pompous."

"You named your horse Destiny," he pointed out, "That's a little grandiose."

"I didn't name him. That was Jaquelle, by way of a joke. 'Where will Destiny take you today?' she would tease me. She doesn't make that many jokes, so I kept the name as a reminder."

"I have never seen such a metal, except once."

"It has been passed down in my family. Just recently, I wrapped the hilt in new leather."

"It's beautiful," Demetrius said.

She smiled coyly, sensing the compliment was not meant only for the sword.

"You said 'except once?'"

"Theodos has one just like it. He's of the line of Evrain, and that sword is an ancient relic from the time of great heroes. Perhaps you are of his line too?"

"What, the descendant of a hero? Of course, but so is every other noble family in the old empire. In Dezearre, swords like this are as common as tortoise roots."

"Then maybe it's not the sword but the hero who wields it."

"Hero," she snorted dismissively. "You know, I was so shocked by what Prince Theodos did, killing his own father. How could King Acheron, a kind man it seems to me, and a good king, have such a son? But then I thought, my parents were a lot like King Acheron, kind and generous and noble, and what kind of a child did they have? Me. At best, I'll be remembered as Ariella the Drunk. And I'm not even an accomplished drinker like Lady Ancarette. She can go on all night and the next day while I fall under the table."

Demetrius chuckled.

"I believe you are more ambitious than you let on," he said, "You're a young noblewoman, a good fighter, so you must be ambitious. You must have some high hopes for the future."

She shrugged, smiling in a mysterious way, which made him believe he was not mistaken.

He caught himself observing his companion with minute closeness. The warm, brown color of her eyes, the few loose strands that escaped the leather thong with which she had tied back her hair... she looked so young and fragile in the flickering fire light.

"You must be only two and twenty," he blurted out.

"I'll have you know," she replied with an amused note in her voice, "I am four and twenty."

"Oh, I beg your pardon," he declared with mock gravity, "I was not aware that I was in the presence of such venerable antiquity. A well-preserved four and twenty to be sure!"

She laughed, and it was a welcome sound to his ears.

He enfolded her in his arm, and she relaxed into him, resting her head on his shoulder. What would happen if he tried to kiss her now that they no longer had their roles to play, he the slave and she the honored guest? Would she push him away in disgust?

She seemed so innocent and trusting, like some free-roaming knight errant of old. As far as he could tell, she really was that pure of heart. The laws of chivalry could be drilled into someone's head to a certain extent, but Demetrius could tell it was in her nature too. The way she had acted towards him on his last night as a slave showed that she took what she wanted, but not if it hurt others. And she had come back for him at the castle wall, when she could have easily escaped. The warmth of her body aroused him, but he did not want to wake her. He considered it more merciful not only for her but also for himself to avoid further entangling their bodies and souls. They would each have to go their separate ways, and even now he felt a sudden sense of loss at the thought.

In the morning, they set out again, taking turns riding Destiny, and sometimes both walking to let the horse have some relief.

Their food supplies were quickly dwindling. Walking and riding gave them both hearty appetites, and by midday all the cured meat Demetrius had brought from the palace were gone. Most of the forest berries had not yet ripened, and there were few to be had.

"I wish I had thought to bring a bow," Demetrius complained. "But in my foolish haste I had forgotten that I don't know how to kill a pickor with my bare hands."

The playful pickors, small and swift as deer, but much more delicious, grazed on the forest mosses and leapt about within easy shooting distance.

"Don't blame yourself," Ariella said, "There was not enough time for thinking, and we barely escaped with our lives."

"There is an inn close to this part of the woods," Demetrius said at length. "We could risk staying the night there and obtaining some food… though it is a place of ill repute."

Ariella considered this. "Perhaps food of ill repute is better than none at all?" she queried.

"I certainly hope so. In any case, we should find no friends of the prince there."

They reached the inn by nightfall. By that time they were weary and hungry enough to risk discovery for the sake of a hot meal and a warm bed.

At first, all they could see of the inn were its lights beyond the shadowy lattice of the forest. Soon, the silhouette of the building and its adjoining stables outlined itself against the darker grey of the night.

"Just one night here," Demetrius said, "and after that we will cut through the Ringing Woods. The prince's men would not follow us there, and beyond it you will be able to cross into Dezearre."

"Have you been here before?" Ariella asked.

"No, but I have heard that the inn is a den of thieves and brigands. Beyond this, the Ringing Woods is rumored to be infested with elves."

"It can't be worse than the palace we just escaped," she shrugged.

CHAPTER 4

Ariella took one final look at the forest that had kept them concealed. She sighed, bracing herself for her return to contact with the human race, her last experience with which was less than stellar.

The sign over the door of the inn was barely readable. It seemed to say "The Married Fiddler," though it was hard to tell.

A boy of about ten came out to meet them and offered to take the horse to the stable. Ariella reluctantly let him lead Destiny away.

"Are you ready?" Demetrius asked.

She wasn't, truly. She wondered if they would share a room, share a bed. It would be cruel to ask him to do something that had only been his duty as a slave. Of course, he had been eager to do it at the time, but her sense of honor forbade her from mentioning it unless he did first.

She nodded. Together, they entered the inn.

At first glance, it did not seem to be a den of thievery and iniquity. The place was fairly clean. The sandy floor strewn with pine branches suffused the dining area with a pleasant smell.

The patrons talked in subdued tones. A couple of them

were dressed like gentlemen, a few others, rough and ready commoners, did not appear too suspicious. Still, she now knew only too well that thieves and traitors could be found in all levels of society.

The boy soon returned and began to confer with a tall, lean, man who wore a bald spot like a point of pride surrounded by long, lank hair. This man then proceeded to fill the customers' glasses and chat with them, and so Ariella believed him to be the owner of the establishment.

"Landlord!" Demetrius called, "All your best food, please. We're hungry."

The bald, long-haired man turned to him and stared for a fraction of a second more than was polite. Then he approached their table.

"Of course you are," he said cheerfully, "I have never had a customer who was not hungry, for this road is long and without many other inns for many miles."

"Yes, we noticed," Ariella remarked.

"The Wheels of Epheor turn, and there is no telling what they will bring into a man's life," the innkeeper pronounced mysteriously, "I see you have traveled far, and as my stable boy tells me, with only one horse… and no saddle."

He paused and stared at the travelers expectantly. They knew he was trying to tell them something but they were too exhausted and hungry to care or understand.

"Perhaps we should talk in a private room," the innkeeper said, "I will have food brought to you."

He led them into a small wood-panelled dining chamber in which the furniture consisted of a small, round table and two chairs. There were not many decorations except a wooden statue depicting an old, wrinkled, and wily-looking creature with a halo of rays flowering out behind him, the god of travelers and thieves.

"Now," the innkeeper said as they seated themselves, "I have eyes. And my eyes tell me you are a noble couple riding away from the royal castle disguised as royal servants. I know not what caused this sudden twist of fate for you, but I do know that by coming here, you bring danger to my establishment."

They were silent, letting him continue.

"I see you don't deny it," he said, "that's good. I like dealing with honest people."

"We can pay you to keep your silence, if that is what you ask," Demetrius said.

"I am an honest innkeeper," he replied, not showing any signs of excitement or greed, "and I will accept payment for the food and lodging I provide. However, if you are pursued by the king's men, and if you wish me to be silent on that account should they come here in search of you... I would require a service. Otherwise, there is no telling what manner of information would leak out..."

"What kind of service?" Ariella asked suspiciously.

The landlord suddenly backed away from the table. "I normally don't ask gentlefolk for such a service. I need your words that you would not try to harm me if I tell you."

"Why are you doing this?" Demetrius asked.

"Because I fear that you would not perform the service unless you had hefty... motivations."

"So now we can't leave here until we have performed the service or you will sell us out?" Ariella asked.

"I'm afraid so," the innkeeper nodded, crossing his arms before his chest.

"All right, just tell us what it is then," Demetrius prompted, "I promise not to hurt you right away."

The innkeeper hesitated, but saw that this was as good a promise as he was going to get.

"I will tell you," he addressed Demetrius, "and then you can tell the lady. Then I shall retreat and allow you to think it over."

"Oh for the blithering stars' sake!" Demetrius shouted. "All right, let me get it over with."

The innkeeper whispered in his ear and then promptly left the room, while Demetrius frowned in perplexity.

"Well, what is it?" Ariella demanded.

"He wants us to do... well, what we did the other night at the palace, but with several people watching."

Ariella was silent for a moment. Her heart suddenly began to beat like a wild drum with both fear and triumph.

"Just watching?" she asked.

"I believe so. He said it was a performance, not an orgy."

"Still..." She couldn't believe she was considering it.

"You don't have to say another word. We will walk out of this room and flee this accursed place. By tomorrow we will be in the forest, where no one will dare follow."

She shook her head and grinned to see how surprised he was.

"It's not anything we haven't done before," she said, "Besides, we need food and rest. We must be prepared for the journey. Who knows what dangers lie ahead in the haunted forest?"

"But... in front of people? Are you sure you want to do this."

"An audience would not be so bad," she said with a grin, daring him.

Demetrius fixed her with a fascinated gaze. "I thought you would be the one to object to this. As for me, I've been a slave long enough to be accustomed to all sorts of depravities. And I suspect that if we don't do this, the honest innkeeper will send an informer to tell the prince exactly where we are."

"I do believe he's honest enough to do it," Ariella agreed.

Even as she said it, they both froze, hearing hoof beats outside. Regular visitors to the inn, or the prince's men? The question was evident on both their faces as they exchanged looks.

In the next instant, the innkeeper burst into the room.

"Under the table, now!" he cried.

Ariella looked perplexedly at the small space under the table, half-concealed by the shabby tablecloth.

"Oh, ye gods!" the innkeeper exclaimed. "Why can't anyone simply do as they're told?"

He hastened over to the table, crouched down and lifted

three floorboards that had previously looked seamlessly intact.

The fugitives did not have to be asked again. They dove into the small opening beneath the floor, and the innkeeper replaced the wooden boards above them.

A small part of the room was still visible through a small crack between the boards, and Ariella could see the merest outline of her companion's face in darkness. She would have shivered in the cold, earthy space in which they were lying if it wasn't for the warmth of his body as she lay snuggled into it and his heavy arm holding her protectively. She struggled not breathe too loudly; it was hard not to when his touch made her skin tingle and her pulse quicken.

Just in time for the guards to enter the dining room, the innkeeper bustled about as if he had been doing nothing less innocuous than setting the silverware on the small table.

A lieutenant of the prince's guard stepped into the room. From below, his close-cropped hair and his face looked stern, thin, and angular.

"So, Vidor, now you're harboring fugitives," the lieutenant declared.

"Ah, Lieutenant Portul, always good to see you," the innkeeper exclaimed.

"I wish I could say the same, but I am not exactly thrilled to revisit your thug-ridden nest."

Vidor tutted. "Then why do you come here looking for fugitives?" he asked, all innocence.

The guard stepped inside with intimidating self-assurance, striding past the innkeeper and peering into the dark corners of the room.

Ariella held her breath. Her eyes used to the darkness now, she could better see the handsome outline of her companion's face. If this was the last thing she would see before she was found and killed, so be it.

"Because just as surely as excrement flows down from the sewers into the river," the guard finally replied, "so all human refuse flows down to your establishment. Sooner or later, they all end up here."

"I would take offense to that if I didn't know you were just a country boy who had listened to too much gossip," Vidor replied. "But since your ears are open, you might have also heard that my place lies outside of King Acheron's grasp. The king's law has no power here."

"King Acheron is dead," the lieutenant retorted.

This was the first thing he said to truly affect the innkeeper. "I am sad to hear it," he finally pronounced. "What happened?"

"The king fell ill suddenly. One of those fevers that come when foul air blows in from the swamps of the north."

"Carrion berry swamps," Vidor muttered. "Who has replaced him?"

"King Theodos."

"I see. I was going to say that out of respect for King Acheron I would let you look around if you so wished, but King Theo?... It doesn't really have a ring to it at all."

"How dare you?" the guard growled.

"I dare," Vidor replied coolly, "because at this moment every single one of your men has an arrow aimed at his eyeball, and my marksmen do not miss."

Ariella saw the lieutenant dart back out into the dining hall to ascertain this. She could not see the men supposedly posted there, but evidently the innkeeper had not been bluffing.

"You would raise your weapons against the king's men?" the lieutenant asked, truly incredulous.

"I already have."

"Lieutenant, we've searched upstairs. They're not here," one of the guards reported from the other room.

"You are lucky," the guard finally stated, his voice heavy with malevolence.

"Oh yes, I know," the innkeeper replied casually. "Now, kindly leave my establishment."

"If I find out that they have been here, we'll return to destroy your nest of vipers."

Footsteps, then the clattering of horse hooves outside. She looked over at Demetrius, who had also been holding his breath all through the last exchange. Now, he finally released it.

"I think they've really gone," he whispered. "Does this mean we owe the innkeeper a favor?"

"Probably so."

They heard footsteps again, and the landlord lifted away the floorboards, filling the little hiding place with golden light.

"Have you decided?" he asked grandly.

"I have one question," Ariella stated. "Will they?... I mean are they going to?..."

"Yes, very likely some will wish to pleasure themselves. But most people are lazy and would rather watch than do," the innkeeper concluded matter-of-factly.

"I want the food first!" Ariella declared savagely.

She clambered out of the hiding place, assisted by Demetrius.

"Of course, my lady!" the innkeeper cooed. "Then we have an agreement?"

Ariella and Demetrius both nodded. It was probably the fact that the place was crawling with Vidor's archers and there was no way of escape anyway.

"Excellent. I will bring you the text."

"There's a text?" Demetrius asked in astonishment.

"Of course. I want my guests to be well entertained."

CHAPTER 5

After a most delicious dinner of roasted pickor meat in the small private room, Ariella felt in better spirits. They set about reading the play which the innkeeper had given them.

She could feel the warmth of Demetrius' body as they sat side by side perusing the text, and she anticipated holding him in her arms again, though the idea that an audience would be present made her nervous. She was strangely impressed with herself for agreeing to this. Was it merely the danger of being sold out to the prince, or did part of her want to do this simply for the pleasure of it? After all, she had been promised three nights of entertainment by a slave, but now that he was a free man, she dared not ask for them.

Ariella was so lost in thought that she had stopped reading.

"This play should certainly amuse the audience," Demetrius commented.

Contrary to their expectations, and much to their relief, the text did not dictate exactly what they should do, but merely provided some preliminary dialogue for the scene they were to act out, leaving the rest to their imagination.

The play was Baconius, Prince of Roanland, but not the original version. It had been rewritten by some bold scribe, perhaps the innkeeper himself, with a happy ending. The parchment they were reading contained the last scene of the play, which traditionally involved the tragic death of Baconius and about twenty other characters. Instead, this particular version of the masterpiece presented a much happier conclusion to the tale, Baconius reuniting with his beloved Aurilia.

Ariella's dialogue was not long, and she had it memorized very quickly. Soon, the innkeeper came back. The hour was close to midnight, and as they were led up a wooden staircase and past a series of doors, she wondered what manner of people had gathered to watch the spectacle.

They were led into a room that was too small to be called a hall but was perhaps the biggest private room the establishment had to offer. There was a dais to the left side of the door, obviously intended as a stage for the performers. It was covered with a velvet blanket and strewn with mismatched cushions. To the right of the door, opposite the stage, the audience sat in a ragged semicircle three rows deep.

About a dozen men and only two women centered all their attention on the couple as they entered. The power of their collective gaze, nearly palpable in its intensity, made Ariella feel naked, exposed, even though she was still very much dressed.

She tried to think of her character. Never having participated in a play herself, she recalled the infrequent times when a wandering company of players, usually lost on the road, stumbled upon her castle. She remembered the players' absolute concentration on their craft. There was not even a hint that the actor on the stage was anyone but the tragic prince he was portraying, or the saucy maid or the treacherous killer, so fully had they transformed into their role.

It seemed Demetrius was similarly committed to the play, for he already stood upon the stage with the lofty yet troubled attitude of Prince Baconius. He looked so handsome and distant, and she wondered whether this was another real side of him, so different from his usual cheerful humor. Not that his cheerful banter ever rang false; it must have been his true nature to be so full of joy and good humour, perhaps what he had been like as a youth; but he had another side, a deeply melancholy one that she was seeing only now as he drew from it for his role. She wondered what sort of lover such a man truly wanted.

"Please welcome the players!" the innkeeper pronounced. "These two mysterious travelers will now present Baconius, Prince of Roanland."

The innkeeper took his seat in the back, motioning for them to begin. The audience shifted, preparing for the spectacle. Ariella spotted a couple of the gentlemen whom she had seen earlier downstairs. There were also a few more men in luxurious attire, perhaps wealthy merchants, and the rest, though not completely unkempt, had the air of common brigands. Of the two women, one was stunningly beautiful and richly arrayed, the other, sitting in the front row, rather comely, and dressed just like the brigand category of men, who wore simple cotton shirts and rough leather vests.

Ariella was supposed to enter onto the stage to begin the scene. Her hands were trembling, but she took a deep breath and commenced walking towards the low stage. One small step brought her up to Demetrius' level, and he pretended he had just sighted her.

"What do I see?" he exclaimed, his smooth voice carrying well to the back rows, but not so loud as to be overwhelming. "Are you a spirit? A ghost sent to torment me for my misdeeds? Why do you take on the shape of one so dearly loved, who has too soon departed from this sad earthly abode?"

He had spoken his lines with great conviction, but then, just for a split second, he dropped his act and winked at her with his right eye, unseen by the audience.

Ariella took another couple of steps towards him.

"I am no spirit," she replied.

"But I received word that you were dead…"

"That is what I wanted everyone to believe. But I did not drown. When I fell in the river, I breathed through a reed and swam away, and then I waited for you to regain your kingdom."

The audience laughed at this facile explanation for Aurilia still being alive.

"I did so," Demetrius continued, unfazed, "and I avenged my father's death. Now we can be together, my beloved."

He embraced her, and suddenly his mouth was claiming hers, and she nearly forgot where she was. After this, the dialogue ended, and it was all up to them. Ariella was breathless, from the kiss and her nerves. But she buried her face in Demetrius' long dark hair, determined to carry on.

"We can do this," he whispered to her.

She squeezed his hand in thanks.

Still hiding her face from the audience, she trailed kisses down his neck. The scent of his skin, which still held whatever perfume it was he had used in the palace, now mingled with sweat and the pine smell of the forest. It enticed her to lick his skin, to lose herself in his kisses and his caresses.

The thought of being watched melted away as passion coursed through her body. She was much more aware of being slowly undressed, the laces of her tunic unwound, of Demetrius removing his silken robe and pressing her against his broad chest.

Slowly, he lowered her to the cushioned, carpeted floor. The audience watched raptly. She was proud of certain contours of her body, such as her breasts, not too big or too small, but beautifully shaped and fitted to her lean frame, and the long, supple muscles of her legs. She liked undressing for a lover, but to have an entire audience riveted by her body was something else entirely, something amazing.

Melting into Demetrius' embrace, she moaned uncontrollably, a prisoner of her own lust, and a witness to the lust of the audience. There was no need to pretend for this play. The woman in the front row licked her lips, devouring the couple with her gaze.

One man in the audience was panting, another, sitting in the third row, was somewhat discreetly touching himself inside his cloak. In other circumstances, it may have been strange or repulsive, but now, seeing his rugged, masculine face, seeing that he was purely a hostage of passion just as she was, Ariella suddenly became aware of being swept away by an even stronger surge of desire.

Little by little, everything shifted. Instead of being oblivious of the audience, she fed off their rapture as they fed off hers. Their gazes caressing her, although it did seem degrading and wrong, at the same time, it gave her the sense of power and the sense of being adored, just as Demetrius did when he made love to her. She drank in their pleasure.

Soon her entire body was exposed to their ravenous gazes. Demetrius leaned over her, his muscular form in all its glory open to the audience, and wanting her. It was not merely a stage act on his part, it couldn't be. Desire drove them on as their bodies merged. He filled her slowly. The pain and pleasure swirled inside her until he penetrated as deep as he possibly could, and then there was only pleasure. He stayed there for a moment, her inner core perfectly molded to him, for just a moment, and then he withdrew, only to enter again with slowly building intensity.

The couple moved together with perfect harmony. She didn't know how, but Demetrius simply seemed to divine what she wanted. She longed for him to thrust even deeper inside her, and as if in response, he took her right leg and lifted it up until it was propped against his shoulder, leaving her open to the deepest possible penetration. She cried out in ecstasy each time he pushed inside her. The whole room became a blur.

His eyes looked into hers, and she sensed that he was completely oblivious to the audience now too, seeking only her pleasure.

She thought he would surely climax, the sparks in his eyes igniting to a frantic light, but instead he withdrew, only to continue the lovemaking with his mouth hot between her thighs.

The audience did not foresee this turn of events, and some cheered to show their appreciation as the scene would be prolonged.

By then, Ariella was nearly deaf to their cries. She closed her eyes, connected to the rest of the world only through his touch.

Gods, it was thrilling!

She suddenly realized she was screaming at the top of her voice, although she was not even close to her peak. It was simply the things he did with his tongue. Each new assault upon her organ shot long tendrils of desire through her body.

Suddenly there were only the flowers of rapture blooming within her as she reached her peak.

"Could you come again?" he whispered in her ear while she recovered, panting in his embrace.

"Yes, I want you inside me," she whispered.

She sat up, and kneeled over him, urging him gently down onto the cushion. She wanted to make love to him now as she had done that night in the palace. But she knew his body better now. Their motions flowed smoothly together. She had the best angle from which to view his muscular form, watching it rock with her motions. She felt his explosive power beneath her.

But that power was now yielding to her. She leaned forward to kiss his lips while he cupped both her breasts, taking full pleasure in possessing them. He was reveling in her aggressive lovemaking as she rose to a level of pure wildness.

She was so close…

She could feel that he was too, and she pumped her hips savagely, her mind empty of anything else but reaching that peak.

Suddenly, he groaned with utter abandon, his body tensing between her legs. It was just enough to push her over the edge. She felt she the entire room slip away as she was transported to a realm of pure pleasure.

Only after resting for a few moments did she slowly become more aware of everyone else around them.

At this point, some people in the audience were cheering. Others simply sat there, panting and not taking their eyes off the couple. Some ran out of the room, perhaps to attend to their own needs in private. Others stood up in ovation, whistled and applauded.

"Thank you, thank you!" Vidor was suddenly up on stage, accepting the applause as if he had just performed a great feat. "As I say, I always do my best entertain my guests. Thank you!"

Before she knew it, Ariella was wrapped up in a great silken cloak handed to her by one of the inn's servants. Together with Demetrius, who was also modestly enfolded in dark fabric, she was ushered by Vidor himself down the hallway and into a guest room.

"Please ring the bell if there is anything you need," the innkeeper said. "And sleep well… I think you will."

He smiled at his own joke and left them, closing the door softly behind him.

Demetrius seemed comfortable as he began bustling about the little room right away, looking for towels. He picked up one of the jugs of water that had been left for them and beckoned her over. Casting off his cloak, in all his unclothed glory, he stepped into a large tub and poured the water over his head, letting it stream down the crags and valleys of his beautiful body. When Ariella joined him, he poured the warm water on her, running his hands along her body and between her legs, washing off the essences of their lovemaking.

Exhausted, Ariella leaned against him.

At last, he spoke. "It wasn't what you expected."

Ariella was stunned. Of course, she suddenly realized, he would know about such things. Perhaps he had once had to perform in exactly during his time as a slave.

"It was terrifying," she admitted, "…but then, much more amazing than I ever hoped."

He lifted her up gently and carried her to the bed. When she was snug beneath the covers, he joined her, taking her hand and interlacing his fingers with hers.

A comfortable silence stretched out between them. Ariella could see the outline of his face and its perfect angles in the darkness. She looked at him intently.

"Did you enjoy it?" she suddenly asked.

"Yes," he replied.

But she couldn't quite read his face.

It reminded her of the time, only two nights ago, when he had answered just as confidently to her question about his willingness to serve her.

"The main reason I went through with it was that I find you irresistible," he added simply.

Ariella hoped he could not feel her heartbeat suddenly race.

"I could say the same thing about you," she replied honestly.

She was careful not to mention her feelings, for she did not know what these were as yet. She could only speak of the magnetic bodily attraction. As for the person, she knew so little about him, and she suspected he held more than one secret, not least of them being his history with Prince Theodos.

"And after all," she continued, "we were meant to spend three nights together if Prince Theodos had not so rudely imposed himself upon our plans."

Demetrius laughed. "Three nights, that is what you wish?"

"Not necessarily," she replied, hoping her voice had a seductive allure, "There are more than three nights of travel ahead of us."

He smiled at her in that cheerful, carefree way he had, just like when they had first met, when there had been no assassins, no growing attachments, and no secrets between them.

"Then I shall fulfil the services I promised," he said, "and maybe even more."

He stroked her cheek softly, and she drew herself closer, wrapping her right arm around him and laying her head on his chest. The thought of 'more' pleased her, but also made her strangely anxious as she wondered whether he meant simply another few nights of making love or something more beyond that.

Ariella did not permit herself to hope for anything more. She had already wasted a year mooning over a handsome guardsman with whom she had a few good times, but who had promptly forgotten her and moved on to a new prize. Somehow, she didn't think that the man lying next to her was at all so careless in giving and withholding his attentions, but she could not know for sure, and after all, she had sworn never to waste time with serious feelings for a man ever again.

One day, she would be married and produce an heir to her barony, but the women of Dezearre dreamed of glory in battle rather than the dresses they would wear on their wedding day.

For the moment, she was content lying in his arms, but just before she fell asleep her imagination created images of Demetrius visiting her castle in Leduryon, walking cheerfully through its halls, meeting Jaquelle, her former nursemaid who was still an important mentor even in her adult years, and dining with them at the main table while the other warriors looked at them and winked at each other and Helnom, the aged captain of the guards sang his usual "Hand me my trusty bow." It was a silly fantasy, she reminded herself, and soon sleep overtook her.

In the morning, they came down to find Vidor already busy making breakfast. He greeted them enthusiastically, as if nothing strange or debauched had passed between them the previous night. The few other guests, three brigand-like characters who may have been at the play the previous night acted like they did not know them.

"I expect you are eager to be on your way," Vidor called out while stirring something that smelled delicious in a large pan.

"We are," Demetrius said. "Thank you for your hospitality. I have never slept better in all my life."

The innkeeper chuckled.

They ate with a hearty appetite the eggs and wild boar bacon that he served up along with large glasses of rowelberry juice.

As they were finishing up, Vidor was called outside by one of his young assistants.

Demetrius and Ariella went out into the morning that held the lightly mouldering grass scent of late summer gradually seeping into autumn to find their host shouting at someone to "get away." He then picked up a rock and hurled it at the trespasser, who was hiding behind a tree not far from the inn. A thick mane of mud-caked red hair made Ariella think at first that it was some kind of beast, but the tangle-tressed figure emerging from behind the tree had a dirty, human face and a sun-browned, scrawny feminine body clothed in tattered rags.

"What– who is that?" Ariella asked.

"That's just a worthless thief," Vidor replied.

"I'm hungry," the creature said from the bushes.

"I don't care!"

Vidor picked up another rock from the ground, but this time Ariella stood between him and his target.

"Please, don't," she said. "Whatever she has done, that is no way to treat a fellow human."

After barely escaping from the palace with her life, Ariella could sympathise with this lowly outcast, who seemed to have no food and no certainty of what tomorrow might bring. Ariella at least had Demetrius for a companion, but this girl had no one.

"You are too kind for your own good, my lady," Vidor huffed, "This one does not deserve your benevolence. She is a fiend with no morals and no rules but selfishness. I had sheltered her before, but she repaid my kindness with ingratitude."

"She looks like she has suffered much," Ariella argued.

"Of course she has," Vidor agreed, "for no one will have dealings with her, the treacherous beast."

Ariella looked at the 'beast' intently, trying to understand how such a pathetic looking creature could be harmful.

"Come here," Ariella called to her.

She did not know what had come over her. Perhaps it was the lovemaking she had experienced the previous night that had made her overly sensitive, or the feeling of being alone in a strange land that made her sympathetic to a poor outcast, but for some reason she could not stop herself from feeling sorry for the wild looking girl in the bushes.

"Come, I just want to talk to you," Ariella called again.

At last, the girl came forth. Now that she was committed to leaving her shelter, she walked bravely on, ignoring the innkeeper whose hand was still clutching the rock.

"Who are you?" Ariella asked gently.

"Mara is my name," the girl replied.

She looked no older than twenty. Her face was sunken and gaunt, but her green eyes, large with hunger, looked unflinchingly at Ariella.

"Mad Dog Mara is what they call her," the innkeeper commented.

"Do you have any family?" Ariella continued.

"I have no mother and father, my lady, for they were killed a long time ago by Koroi raiders."

"So you are all alone?"

"Yes, my lady," she replied, "but I am well able to fend for myself. If only someone would give me a decent meal, I could work to earn my keep."

"Ha! That was exactly what she said to me, just before she tried to steal from my jewel box," Vidor chimed in.

Mara bit her lip and said nothing.

Despite this revelation, Ariella felt her heart flood with pity for the poor girl.

"She looks so starved. It may have been an act of desperation. Perhaps I could at least give her some food as she asks?"

"An act of treachery was what it was," Vidor insisted. "Do not associate yourself with her, my lady. She is a bad egg. She may look miserable and starved now, but it's better to keep her that way. If she had just a little more strength, she would rob us blind, cut our hamstrings, and leave us for the vultures."

Ariella had a hunch that he was right. There was a wilful spirit hidden beneath a façade of humility in that dirty countenance behind its curtain of mud-caked hair.

"Nevertheless, I would like to give her at least something to eat," she insisted, "I cannot bear to see her suffer like this."

"If you so wish," the innkeeper relented, "but she is not

entering my doors again. Come, you can pick out some morsels for her if you like."

Demetrius leaned against the doorway, grinning. Ariella caught him and the innkeeper exchange a knowing look that could have probably been summarized as "women!"

"Aside from that, I will give you plenty of food to take with you," Vidor said, "Who knows when you'll next encounter a hospitable inn like mine?"

He packed a bag full of pickor jerky, goat cheese, and apples, adding a wineskin and handing the lot to Demetrius. Ariella proffered several silver Rals to pay for their food and their stay, but Vidor waved them away.

"No need! You have more than paid for your food and lodging with last night's performance. I dare say I made quite a profit! And as I said, I am an honest man. I have my code of honor, though you may not think much of it. I will do everything in my power to cover your tracks and delay your pursuers."

"That would be too much to ask," Ariella replied. "Do not put yourself in danger. It seems Prince Theodos isn't one to take defeat lightly, and I would not want his vengeance to fall upon you."

"Fear not, my lady," the innkeeper said with a confident smile, "Though my inn is officially within the prince's domain, it has never bowed to royal laws."

Ariella could not help but hold some grudging admiration for the man. Despite their being all but enslaved to him a few hours earlier, it was a strangely cordial parting.

The innkeeper even went as far as to walk them out.

Mad Dog Mara waited outside, sitting back on her heels in what was probably supposed to appear a stoic pose beneath a tree.

Ariella handed her a piece of bread, which she immediately devoured.

"My lady, good sir," the girl began, "Please give me leave to accompany you on your journey."

"Now look what you've done," Vidor remarked.

"Our journey is dangerous," Demetrius said, looking down at the girl with pity. "It's only for those in desperate straits."

Mad Dog Mara sat back on the ground and laughed. It was a hysterical sound, indicative of her nickname.

"And what do I look like to you?" she cried, clutching the rags that served as her clothing. "Queen of the Wonder Realms?"

"You are not heading through the Ringing Woods, are you?" Vidor suddenly queried.

Ariella and Demetrius quickly exchanged glances. After all that had transpired, Ariella thought they could confide in the innkeeper with the secret of their destination, though Mad Dog Mara seemed decidedly less trustworthy.

They stepped away from the red-haired girl, and talked to Vidor in low tones.

"We are heading for the Woods," Demetrius said. "It is the shortest route, and the one where Theodos's guards are least likely to follow."

"But that's insane," Vidor replied. "I know it may seem the more direct route, but I pray you do not go that way. The elves never let anyone pass unnoticed, and when you're in the company of elves, well... they play tricks on your mind, and I don't mean in a good way."

Demetrius did not seem surprised by this information, though he was not completely unconcerned.

"It may be our only chance," he stated.

A noise alerted Ariella, and she spun around to see Mara crawling on her hands and knees across the dusty courtyard towards them.

"Please, please, take me with you. I won't betray you," she pleaded with tears in her voice, though none had yet appeared in her eyes.

"What do you think?" Ariella wondered, turning to Demetrius.

His lips twisted to one side in a crooked smile, and he shrugged. "Since she's as desperate as we are, and the gods have put her in our path, and your heart aches for her...

Maybe it's fate."

CHAPTER 6

Long before noon, they rode away from the inn on two horses: Destiny, and a chestnut nag they bought from Vidor. The latter horse was named Mock, a name evidently given to describe what he did with the concept of running, and was worth exactly the pittance they had paid for him. They had little choice, as Mock had been the only horse available for sale, and Vidor had thrown in a saddle and bridle for Destiny as well.

Demetrius, who had to ride the sorry beast with Mara sitting behind him, was nevertheless in good spirits. He prattled on about the pleasures of the open road, while Mara gladly agreed with everything he said. Ariella did not regret her decision to take Mara along, but nevertheless she watched her new companion suspiciously.

The way Mara's fingers wove around Demetrius' chest was too sensuous for her liking. They were not merely holding on for support but sometimes furtively caressing his torso and his shoulders. Demetrius was wearing that wry smile of amusement again.

Ariella was slightly angry at herself for feeling jealous. She could tell Demetrius was not taking the girl seriously, but even if he had been, would she have any right to feel betrayed?

Still, she could not contain her anger as the man she had caressed only hours ago was held by another. She could not watch for one moment longer. She pulled gently on the reins to halt Destiny, and the other horse stopped out of laziness and habit.

"Your horse is tiring," Ariella declared. "Two riders are too much for him. Mara, you ride Destiny, and I shall walk."

"No, I can walk," Demetrius offered gallantly.

To Ariella's surprise, Mara seemed happy to oblige. She sprang down and with Ariella helping lift her up into the saddle, she proudly sat up and smiled with a most wicked look.

Demetrius also dismounted from Mock, but as soon as he did, Mara squeezed Destiny's flanks with her heels and trotted off. Then she kicked the horse's flanks, leaning forward and goading it into a gallop.

"Mara! What are you doing?" Ariella cried, but realized all too late that Mara was quite casually stealing her horse.

"I can catch her," Demetrius resolved, placing his foot in the stirrup to mount Mock.

Ariella put her hand on his shoulder to halt him.

"Wait," she said, her mouth struggling against a mischievous grin.

"He's truly amazingly fast," Demetrius remarked.

Destiny sped up, galloping away at a mad dash. He was about to disappear around a turn in the forest path, and it was only then that Ariella put two fingers in her mouth and gave a resounding whistle.

Destiny skidded to a halt and came galloping back towards Ariella. Mara screamed with fury and pulled on Destiny's mane, trying to change his direction, but no matter what Mara did, the horse never veered off course, until it slowed down and circled around to Ariella's side, tucking its nose into her neck.

Mara looked horrified as she met Ariella's flaming gaze. The miscreant jumped off the horse and tried to run, but she did not take two steps before Demetrius caught her. She squirmed and cursed, but he managed to seize both her arms and held them tightly.

"Please don't kill me!" Mara cried, "Let me go. I won't hinder you none. Just let me go!"

Ariella drew her sword, feeling slightly guilty for taking advantage of the girl's fear. But she wanted her attention, and this seemed like a good way to get it. She tipped the sword towards Mara's neck and used its point to lift her chin.

"Look at me," she commanded in an icy tone. Tearful green eyes filled with despair looked into hers.

"You want me to spare your life?" Ariella asked. "Do you realize that you just tried to steal a horse whose sires had been bred by my ancestors for generations, a horse that is worth much more than your miserable life? You want me to let you go? So you can run back down the road and betray us to Theodos's guards?"

"No, my lady. I would do no such thing."

"Is that the truth, Mara?"

"I don't know…" Mara sobbed. "Please spare me."

"You don't know because you don't think very far ahead," Ariella continued sternly. "Now listen to me well. I will spare your life, but you are not leaving our side. You asked to come on this journey, so come you shall."

"Please, let me go, my lady. I am of no use to you."

"Silence! You may have overheard us talking to Vidor, so you may know that we're fugitives. Our lives are in danger every second that we stay in Chaldea. We cannot afford to let you go now that you know our secret. If I see you trying to take so much as five paces away from us, I will kill you. Is that clear?"

Mara nodded.

"Now, you may walk alongside us while we ride."

Demetrius looked a little stunned, though he could not repress an amused grin as he mounted his nag with promptness, as if he too had been reprimanded.

"And one more thing," Ariella added before riding on, "Never grovel. If I had a mind to kill you, I would have, and your groveling would not have prevented me. Humans are vulnerable creatures, that much is true, but the least we can do is die with dignity if that is our fate."

As soon as Ariella mounted Destiny, the horses walked on, Mara sobbing and trudging beside them.

Demetrius was silent for a few moments, then he said. "Remind me never to make you angry."

Ariella flashed him a quick smile but then reverted to a stern demeanor for Mara's sake.

"Don't ever try to steal my horse," she replied.

And don't try to steal my heart. It was a foolish thought, she told herself. How could she feel anything for someone she barely knew?

After a brief time, Mara grew cheerful, perhaps due to realizing that she would not be killed. She wiped away her tears. Her face blossomed into a mischievous grin.

"Did you see one of Vidor's 'plays'?" she suddenly asked.

They both hesitated to answer, exchanging nervous looks. Mara's full lips stretched in an even wider grin.

"You did!" she exclaimed. "Maybe you even acted in one?"

Ariella did not know what to say until Demetrius burst out laughing.

"Yes, we acted in one," Ariella admitted, "and we were very good."

"Fancy that!" Mara exclaimed with glee, "a high-born lady like yourself being reduced to whoring for money."

Ariella refused to take the bait and remained perfectly calm.

"We didn't do it for money," Demetrius stepped in, and Ariella shot him a grateful look, "We needed shelter from our enemies. And besides, it was not whoring but a work of art. I had never seen Baconius done so well."

"The happy ending rather suits it," Ariella added.

"Well, I was in Rubius and Marcella once," Mara volunteered. "And I mean at the inn, not in a theater or nothing."

Demetrius raised an eyebrow. "Was there a happy ending on that one too?"

"It was a very happy ending," Mara said. "I never had such

a good spanking in my life."

"That is definitely a different ending than the one I remember," Ariella commented.

"We still had to sing, though," Mara went on, "You know, it's not just anyone that can act in Vidor's plays. You've got to have talent and the like."

"I'm sure you were wonderful," Ariella said, seeking conciliation.

"Would you like to hear a song?" Mara asked.

Then, without waiting for a reply, she began:

There was a shepherd good and stout
Who had a lady lover.
He ventured once to take her out
Among the fresh green clover

He laid her on the clover bed
And then took off his trousers
"My lover," said she, turning red
"I haven't got my bowser!"

"Such petty things I pay no mind,"
Replied the shepherd smartly,
So he did enter from behind
And proved himself most courtly.

Ariella had never heard such a crude song in her life, but she applauded politely, and Demetrius joined her.

Mara received the applause as her due, nor did the fount of poetry run dry there. She continued to display her knowledge of folklore, singing five more songs on the same subject.

Despite the lack of sophistication on Mara's part, the singing seemed to lift everyone's spirit, even when they turned off the main path and entered the shadowy forest domain along a narrow trail that was to lead them through the Ringing Woods.

Echoing bird cries haunted the treetops. The travelers

would often look up to see a crow, or just the shadow of a crow, pass overhead.

The forest that they had just traversed was teeming with life, and the one they were entering likewise did, but with a hidden and darker existence. It was not until evening that they saw more signs of it, when an eerie glow seeped among the tree branches.

"There are faces in the trees," Mara suddenly said, looking disgusted.

Ariella looked where Mara was pointing and saw something resembling a face. In the glowing aura surrounding the tree, its features danced and morphed wildly, but there were certainly eyes and a nose and a large, hideous mouth. The travelers stared, transfixed, as the mouth opened, and a strange music issued. Its whine echoed through the forest, sometimes moaning and sometimes wailing. The plaintive tones of the song were picked up by more voices as more and more trees were lit up with ghostly lights.

"Hey there, fellow," Demetrius addressed one of them in his usual cheerful way.

The tree creature did not respond in words, but one of its ever-shifting eyes winked. It was hard to tell whether it was deliberate or simply part of its constantly moving physiognomy.

"This is not the kind of music you want to hear when you're traveling through a dark forest," Mara complained.

"Tell that to the tree spirits," Demetrius muttered.

Mara opened her mouth as if to sing one of her bawdy songs, but did not dare to.

Ariella remarked, "And yet it's strangely beautiful."

"Well, since they ignore us and seem to mean us no harm, I suppose we can go on," Demetrius suggested.

There were glowing trees all around them, and the travelers decided that it was not likely that they would reach a less eerie spot anytime soon. So they found a small clearing and built a fire, hoping that the spirits would not change their calm disposition during the night.

As the branches crackled in the flame and the weary travelers ate, it seemed the tree spirits and other creatures of the forest still took no interest in the human visitors. Mara was nervous at first, but she soon lay down to sleep on the other side of the fire from her two companions.

"I've been puzzling over it all day," Demetrius said. "Aside from her entertainment capability, which is remarkable, Mara is not exactly what I would call an asset. And as for the possibility of her selling us out, I doubt anyone would listen to her even if she did try to betray us to Theodos's men. Did you decide to keep her with us just to teach her a lesson?"

"I'm not sure if there is a lesson in all this," Ariella replied, "but I have to try. If I let her go, she will perish one way or another. But if she sees our journey through, she may gain something in the trials and the suffering of it."

Demetrius looked pensively into the fire. "Does one always learn from suffering?"

"I don't know," Ariella sighed, "eventually, maybe one does."

She looked over at him and suddenly grew concerned. "Demetrius, I'm sorry. I did not mean that your years of slavery were as useful as attending some sort of a learning institution."

He chuckled, and his warm smile let her know he was not upset at her words.

"It certainly was not," he smirked. But just for an instant, his face acquired a somber look. Something haunted him, some long-ago inflicted pain revealed in his sky-blue eyes, "and there are some sufferings that we all undergo with no rhyme or reason, and nothing useful comes of it as far as I can see."

"You always said that your duties were light," Ariella began, "but I'm sure you are just painting a rosy picture for my benefit. I know you haven't known me very long... but if you wish, you can confide in me about your former life. I feel that something weighs heavy on you."

He was silent for a while, considering this.

"There were certainly some scenes that I would rather

forget," he admitted, "But mostly, I was left alone. I had duties similar to the one I performed for you, but the king never obliged me to do them. I always had a choice."

"So you chose… to do that duty for me?" she asked haltingly.

"When you sat with the king at the grand dinner, I was allowed to observe you through a secret curtain. The moment I laid eyes on you, I thought, yes, not only do I agree to do the duty, I wish it with all my heart. Nevertheless, you didn't know that. You didn't know I had the power to choose, and you showed concern for me that night. I will never forget it."

"It was only the decent thing to do… before becoming indecent," she flicked him a roguish smile.

He smiled back, running his hand over his stubble-studded jaw, and the memory of indecent doings added a spark to his eyes. She felt her blood rushing faster from that look alone.

Ariella wanted to know more about the terrible 'scenes' he mentioned, but thought it better not to pry. She decided to ask more general questions instead and hoped he would eventually trust her enough to reveal more.

"It sounds like you were very favored by the king," she offered.

"Oh yes, the king took a liking to me. But when you're favored by the king, you're not favored by anyone else. You must know that, being in favor with Queen Esclarimonde."

"Me?!" Ariella exclaimed. "I am hardly… at least, I don't think so. I've been at court quite rarely. I've spent most of my life at my estate, or patrolling the eastern borderlands as part of my service. I fought in a few skirmishes here and there against the Koroi."

"Then you must have distinguished yourself," he said, "You fight well."

"A little," she said, embarrassed by the compliment.

"Surely your skills as a Zaliati warrior are at least valued?" he asked.

Now Ariella got the sense that he was trying to win her confidence and learn her secrets, but she truly did not know what he was talking about.

"A what warrior?" she asked in confusion.

"Oh, I forgot. You don't know. But you have the skills," he insisted, "When we leapt off the castle wall and you fractioned that crystal to make a bridge for us, that was a magic only known to the very few, the descendants of ancient heroes, or the inheritors of their reincarnated spirits."

"I know that in my family history there are legends that we are descended from the ancient hero, Evrain. But these are just tales. It was only my old nursemaid who taught me to use the crystal. She dabbles in magic."

"Dabbles?" Demetrius huffed. "Clearly, your beloved nursemaid is not telling you everything."

Ariella mused on this a moment. "Then I think she must have a good reason to keep it a secret."

She felt his eyes fixed intensely on her, and she met his hard stare.

At last, he spoke. "Ariella, when you return home... be careful."

She sat up, surprised by his grave tone. "Why?"

"I don't know. But I suspect that the queen knows you are Zaliati, one of the invincible warriors."

"So what if she does?"

"She may be using you in some sort of ploy, in the best case. Or, in the worst, she is trying to eliminate you altogether. You are the descendant of Evrain. That sword may have belonged to his daughter, Yerra. Although Queen Esclairmonde's line has gained control of more and more land through the centuries, you could be the true heir to the kingdom... maybe even the empire."

"But why would the queen?..." Suddenly, Ariella truly felt uneasy. "You mean she sent me here, knowing they would try to kill me?"

He shrugged. "I can't know that for certain, but it is possible. I do not mean to alarm you. I just think you should be on your guard."

"I will travel by way of my castle at Leduryon and take

some of my warriors with me before I report to the queen."

"A wise precaution," Demetrius said. His jaw looked tense as if he was struggling with something. At length, he said, "I wish I did not have to go home. I wish I could make sure you are safe."

This was the first time he showed he truly cared about her, not just because they were traveling companions who had to protect each other for the group's safety. But then, she realized he had already shown signs of caring about her in the small courtesies he performed, and even in the way he made love to her.

"I shall be all right, especially if I am a Zaliati warrior," she winked at him playfully.

"Still, I would like to help," he said. "Once I have returned to my family and they know I'm free, I will visit you, if I may?"

"Of course you may," she replied.

"Then I promise it."

Ariella was astounded. She had the feeling that he meant what he said. Still, this was but the flimsy promise of a man. She did not want to be swayed by it, no matter how deeply and sincerely his blue eyes gazed into hers.

He leaned towards her, and she could smell the alluring scent of his skin.

The next moment, she was falling into a kiss, unable to resist the temptation of his closeness. Her body sprang to life everywhere he touched her – down the right side of her back, up her arm and the back of her head.

She pulled away in hesitation, looking across the flickering embers to where Mara was resting.

"Are you afraid that Mara will write a song about us?" Demetrius teased.

"As a matter of fact I am. I don't think she is as sound asleep as she pretends to be."

"Mara…" Demetrius called softly.

"Don't!" Ariella laughed, "She may think we want her to join us."

Mara did not move, breathing deeply as one in a state of

profound slumber.

"In any case," Demetrius remarked, "I think she is either asleep or pretending well enough for us to continue."

Ariella burst out laughing. Demetrius took advantage of this to pull her down on top of him, and this time Ariella could not resist kissing him, while laughter still coursed through her body.

She saw a sudden movement on the other side of the fire. It was Mara, who sprang up from where she had been lying.

"Riders," Mara said softly, her slight body tense with fear, "I hear riders."

CHAPTER 7

Interrupted in mid-embrace, Demetrius did not feel embarrassed, for he was much too alarmed by Mara's words. He put his ear to the ground, releasing his hold on Ariella as she tried to gracefully roll off him and do the same.

He heard it, a sound like many distant peals of thunder. Riders approaching at speed.

"Let's saddle the horses!" he said.

Ariella sprang into action, and Mara tried to help as best she could, calming and stroking Destiny while he was being saddled. The horse seemed to have found the humans' alarm contagious, or maybe he too sensed the approach of the enemy; he pulled back his ears and pranced nervously.

"Mara, you ride with me," Ariella commanded.

"How on earth are they able to track us at night?" Demetrius wondered.

"I don't know," Ariella replied as she adjusted the saddle girth, "It would have to be some sort of magic."

Meanwhile, Demetrius had saddled his little nag. He mounted it, while Ariella climbed onto Destiny and pulled Mara up. He noted that in a protective gesture she had the girl sit in front of her, safer from any arrows that may fly at them from behind. Mara seemed to weigh almost nothing at all judging by how easily Ariella lifted her onto the horse, but Demetrius was still worried about Destiny carrying the weight of two people when their lives depended on the horses' speed.

They were off, riding through the forest, which was still suffused in the twilight of the tree spirits. The horses galloped, threading their way among the ghostly trees, finding their footing among treacherous roots, and leaping over fallen logs.

The moon peeked through a net of ragged clouds. It illuminated the forest with even more pale brilliance than the ghostly light of the trees.

Destiny, who was carrying two riders, and Mock, who was not very strong to begin with, began to tire. They struggled up a hill, and the riders let them slow down a little. When they reached the peak, the horses breathing raggedly, Demetrius looked back to see whether he could spot their pursuers. And there, among the shimmering forest, he saw them. Black shapes moving through the silvery light. Unmistakably, several riders were heading directly in pursuit of them.

"I didn't think they would follow us into the Ringing Woods," Ariella said. "And yet here they are."

"These are but the outskirts," Demetrius replied, "They won't dare pursue us into the depth of it."

"From what I can see, they look pretty determined," Mara stated.

"Then we ride on!" Ariella concluded.

They cantered wildly down the hill and back into the cover of the forest. Ariella let Destiny run at an easy pace so as not to tire him out completely. Demetrius matched his speed to hers, and he sensed that Mock was grateful.

But all too soon, much sooner than he had expected, he heard the gallop of the pursuers behind him. Glancing back, he thought he saw them, rushing onward through the trees. All of a sudden, he heard a voice he recognized.

"They're not getting away! Onwards!" it cried.

His blood suddenly turned to ice within his veins. It was a voice he hated, a voice he had not expected to hear in this wilderness. Prince Theodos.

But this time, Demetrius knew that no matter how much a small part of him cried out for vengeance, even if it was suicidal, that he would never turn his horse around to charge the prince. He would not give in to hate as he had done in the palace courtyard. There were two women with him now who trusted him, and whom he had come to know and care about in these last few days. To leave them would be unthinkable.

He rode on, quickly looking over at Ariella and seeing by the hard set of her jaw that she too had recognized the voice. Her countenance showed nothing but grim determination.

Demetrius spurred his horse on. This was their last chance for escape, for surely Theodos would not be mad enough to try to enter the Wilderness. But then again, if he had pursued them this far… Demetrius did not want to think about the implications. They would have to ride hard, but if that failed, he was determined to stand and fight, for if he was to be killed, at least he would take Theodos down with him.

"They're catching up!" Mara cried.

Demetrius didn't want to look back, but he saw that it was worse than he had expected. He could now distinguish Theodos's form at the front of his men, who were not far behind.

They were within bowshot. It was only the abundance of trees that saved the fugitives from a hail of arrows. The prince's men were not letting fly, for it would have been impossible to hit a target other than the ghostly forest, and perhaps they feared the consequences of disturbing the forest and its magical beings.

For a moment, Demetrius thought he saw movement at his side. Instinctively, he drew his sword. It seemed that the guards had outflanked them and were coming from a different direction, but when he turned to look, there was nothing, only the usual trees whipping by.

"We should stand and fight, sell our lives dearly," Ariella shouted.

Demetrius agreed, and he was about to slow his horse, when something scorched through his back with excruciating pain. One of the guards had gotten close enough to shoot an arrow. The others were swiftly gaining on them.

Ariella looked over at him anxiously, and now the physical agony was nothing compared to the torment of that cruel thought that he may be too weak to fight. The wound was draining his blood; he could feel its unpleasantly warm trickle down his back.

But with a desperate effort, he gathered his courage. This could not be his ignoble end, Demetrius decided. The least he could do now was to kill as many of the bastards as possible.

Ariella drew her sword.

"Can you fight?" she asked Demetrius.

"I must," he replied.

Then, Demetrius saw that strange movement again to his right. This time he definitely knew it was not the guards. Something was moving through the trees alongside him. The same thing was happening on Ariella's left. He pointed towards it, and she nodded to show that she saw it too.

Vague shapes were following them like shadows, but they were not shadows. They had their own colors, mostly grey and green, and even some semblance of physical shape. It was clear they were not merely ghosts or spirits.

An arrow whistled by Destiny, so close to the horse that it whinnied.

Suddenly, another arrow flew overhead, but it had been shot from somewhere in the depths of the forest, the direction towards which they were riding. Behind them, the guard who was the closest in pursuit fell out of his saddle.

Nothing was visible in the forest ahead, no man or beast who could have shot that arrow. Demetrius looked to his right again, and this time, the outlines of the thing passing became clearer. It was some kind of creature resembling a human, mounted on a horse, but it did not ride like humans rode; it seemed to pass through the trees as if both horse and rider were incorporeal. Its horse was not quite like their horses; it was swanlike in grace and slenderness, even more beautifully proportioned than Destiny.

The rider's face was lean, his grey eyes large and luminous, reflecting the silver of the moon.

"Do not fear," the rider said, "I am Larkos, King of the Elves, and I am riding with you."

For the first time, Demetrius felt a small spark of hope ignite within him.

"Are they your archers up ahead?" Demetrius asked.

"Yes," Larkos replied.

Beside him, elven warriors rode, and on Ariella's other side there were likewise a few riders rippling through the forest like shadows passing over the ocean. She nodded to them and spurred Destiny on. The same hope that Demetrius felt now flashed in her eyes. The horses renewed their efforts, their hooves hammering the forest floor. They sensed their owners' rise in spirit, and they strove harder for every inch of ground.

A whole swarm of arrows flew over the fugitives' heads, digging into the ground just in front of Theodos, and wounding three of his men. The prince dodged one arrow, and pulled on the reins to slow his horse down.

"I will face them now," said the king of the elves.

The elfin host wheeled around, and as they turned they became more palpable. A brilliant light surrounded the king, and he looked magnificent and awe-inspiring.

"These fugitives are mine, elf!" Theodos shouted to him, "Hand them over to me, and our two people shall live in peace."

"No," said the elf king, and his voice shook the entire foundation of the forest.

"I will take them, as is my right," Theodos insisted.

Then Theodos fell into an uneasy silence as the elf king looked at him searchingly.

"You are Zaliati," said the elf king, "but young and untrained. Think: do you dare go up against the king of the elves?"

Theodos hesitated, while his horse retreated a few steps.

"We'll meet again!" the prince shouted, "Perhaps when I have reached full strength, I will dare!"

"If you so wish," said the king softly.

The prince signalled for his guards to retreat, and slowly he turned his horse about, glaring at the fugitives for as long as possible before he rode away.

"Come! They will not return," said Larkos. "You'll be safe here, and your wound will be tended to."

The fugitives followed him in a daze. It seemed the elves were sympathetic to them, but how long before they began to play games with their mind, as Vidor had warned? Perhaps Vidor was completely wrong about these forest dwellers, or so Demetrius hoped. The elf king's words about Theodos being Zaliati still echoed in his ears. Maybe, like Ariella, Theodos had but recently found out about his gift. Maybe that was how he could track them, by sensing another Zaliati warrior's presence in the wilderness. If he had already begun his training, there was no telling how powerful he would become.

They rode a very short distance until they emerged onto a moonlit glade. Here they saw the archers that had made the volley against Theodos. A cluster of circular cabins made in the elfin style out of lithe branches and leaves stood a little farther off.

"We thank you," Demetrius began.

"Yes, without your help, we would have been dead," Ariella added.

Mara just stared at everything, her green eyes wide with awe.

"It is nothing," said Larkos, "but we had better see to your wound. Are you able to dismount?"

Demetrius groaned as he did so. Now that the excitement of the chase was over, and he no longer needed to rally all his strength, he began to feel the effects of his blood loss. In a sudden fit of dizziness, he sank down on the grass beside his horse.

"Theodre!" Larkos called, "Help him."

One of the riders, a golden-haired elf, dismounted and kneeled down by Demetrius. Ariella and Mara also hurried over, looking at him with concern.

The elfin healer whom the king called Theodre said, "The wound is not life-threatening, but let me take him to one of the shelters to be treated."

Demetrius was grateful for the elf's idea, for he was somewhat embarrassed by his wound being the focus of everyone's attention. He felt badly enough as it was, with the arrow sticking out of his back as if he were a one-quilled porcupine.

Theodre led him to one of the circular cabins that stood in the clearing as Mara and Ariella followed the other elves.

The cabin had a pleasant smell of tree boughs. It was like being inside a basket woven of slender branches, and thatched with large leaves.

Something grandiose stood in the middle of the room. It looked like a bed made of flowers, leaves, and twigs. The interlaced twigs formed the bottom layer, the leaf-covered blossoms decorated the top, but the whole thing, as well as each individual component, seemed to be floating in the air.

"Lie down and rest," Theodre said, "And I will remove the arrow."

The bed looked so inviting that Demetrius cared not if it was some monstrous trick the elves were about to play on him. He sunk gratefully onto the flowery canopy. It felt exactly as good as it looked. Flower petals brushed his face, an airy lightness supported him, as if he were floating in the midst of the room. At the same time, his body felt weighed down with fatigue. Sleep descended on him like a bird of prey.

When he awoke, the pain in his back was very mild compared to what it had been before, what felt like just seconds ago.

"It is done," Theodre's silky voice flowed into his consciousness.

"How long was I asleep?" Demetrius asked, his voice hoarse.

"Not long," replied the elf. "I have removed the arrow, and now you will need more rest. But first, I believe your friends wish to see you."

Demetrius rose up on an elbow, just in time to greet Mara and Ariella as they entered the tent. As soon as they saw him, their expressions relaxed. Ariella rushed over to him and embraced him.

"I hope it wasn't too painful?" she asked, frowning with concern.

"No," he replied, "I felt nothing at all. It must have been some elf magic."

"Will he be well enough to hunt tomorrow?" Larkos asked Theodre.

"Of course," said the healer.

"Why are you doing this?" Mara suddenly demanded. She was staring unflinchingly at the elf king. "Why did you help us, and not the other fellows?"

Demetrius and Ariella looked at her with a renewed sense of respect, then smiled at each other. Neither had expected her to be so perceptive, nor so brave.

"The leader of the men who were chasing you… he was wrapped in a cloud of evil," the elf king replied. "I felt the imprint of a dreadful deed upon him, one that cannot be easily forgiven or erased. Besides," he added airily, "I just didn't like the look of him."

"And you like the look of us?" Mara asked, narrowing her eyes.

Larkos took time to consider this question. As he regarded Mara and her two companions in turn, his silvery grey eyes showed some mysterious thoughts.

His gaze came to rest on Ariella.

"You, my dear, are beyond reproach," he said to her. "As for you two…" he turned to Mara and Demetrius, "Well, we shall see what you're made of. Tomorrow, when you will all hunt with us."

CHAPTER 8

Demetrius did not particularly like to hunt. Although he ate meat and recognized that humans were not alone in killing animals just as meat-eating animals killed grass-eating ones, he was often left shaken by the scene of an animal's death. Still, if the elves insisted on a hunt, it was but a small way to repay them for their kindness.

As Demetrius rose from his fragrant bed in the elf cabin, he could not help but recall Vidor's warning about mind games. Still, he reminded himself, the elves had kept them all safe, and mind games, after all, were all in the mind. If they felt so inclined, let them play games. It wouldn't kill anyone.

His wound did not ache as it had the previous night. He felt a very dull and distant throb, more like an itch that takes over when a wound is nearly healed. There were soft, light bandages wrapped around his torso. They had a pleasant smell of herbs and something reminiscent of the mustiness of the forest. Beside his clothes from the palace, he found elven clothes that he assumed were meant for him. Here were riding boots, a beautiful green tunic and grey hose. He quickly put them on, relieved that he was free of the old clothes he had worn in his servitude.

He left the cabin. In the rays of the morning sun, he beheld the elves gathering and greeting each other. They frolicked about like children. One young female performed a series of handsprings all the way across the clearing. A young male somersaulted with apparent ease. Another male threw three colorful disks the size of dinner plates high in the air. He then drew his sword, jumped, spun around and sliced through each disk, cleaving them in half before they fell to the ground. The others applauded. The sound of laughter came from all around. Invisible chimes, helped by the breeze, spread their lovely sounds through the glade.

Among the gambolling elves, he suddenly caught sight of Ariella. She was comparing sword thrusts and parries with one of the youngsters while Mara flirted with another. He noted the envious looks Ariella cast upon Mara, who was freshly attired in the elfin style. The elves must have taken pity on her and given her that finely woven green tunic to replace her rags. Ariella's own clothing was perfectly serviceable and flattered her lean figure, but she cast longing glances upon the finely crafted fabric worn by her companion.

Still, all in all, Ariella looked happy. Suddenly, against all reason, he wished he could take her to his castle and be with her and bask in her happiness every day. He wondered if there was a young man waiting anxiously for her back in Leduryon, perhaps planning an engagement. Surely, such beauty was not without admirers. He caught himself wishing he were the one who would one day be her suitor, but that was only an impossible dream.

"Shall we ride?" a voice said.

Demetrius turned to find the elf king standing at his side. The king was a bit taller than him, but leaner, though his strength was probably not to be judged by mere physical size.

"If you wish, Your Majesty." Demetrius said, "But what are we hunting?"

"The Beolfia," replied the king, "a fabulous beast that dwells only within this forest. It is a wily creature, mighty in its magic power."

Demetrius thought that it may be foolhardy to try to hunt

such an animal, but said nothing in case the elven king was testing his bravery.

"What weapon will you choose? A bow, or perhaps a spear?" Larkos asked.

At this moment, Ariella and Mara came over to them.

"You look well enough!" Ariella exclaimed. "Theodre has worked a miracle."

"I'm glad you have recovered, Demetrius," Mara said, gazing at him beguilingly. "For we would have been bored without you."

Her hair had been meticulously brushed and now shone like burnished red gold.

"I certainly would have been bored without the two of you," Demetrius replied, but without any suggestive inflections. "I will take a spear if I may," he said to Larkos.

"And so will I," Ariella said. "It has been a while since I have thrown a spear, and I could use the exercise."

"I'd like a bow, if you please, your majesty," said Mara.

"Keep in mind," Larkos said, "that the Beolfia can never be killed with any of these weapons."

"Can we at least slow it down?" Ariella asked.

"Maybe," Larkos replied, a mysterious glint in his eye. "But my people usually face it in unarmed combat."

"How can such a creature be defeated?" Mara asked.

"It cannot be defeated, really," Larkos said with a nonchalant air.

As the elves were still preparing for the hunt, most of them being more interested in play-fighting and gambolling, Demetrius decided to practice throwing his spear. The weapon he was given was made by elves, and its fine craftsmanship could not be denied. It felt smooth and springy in his hand, ready to be thrown.

"Shall we join the others?" he asked Ariella.

She nodded. They approached a group of elves who were likewise practicing with their weapons. A circular yellow target stood on the other side of the glade, and the elves proved their accuracy by riddling it with spears and arrows.

When they saw their three guests approaching, the elves politely stepped aside to make room for them. Demetrius was the first to try the target. He judged the distance fairly long, and threw the spear with all his strength.

It greatly overshot its target and lodged itself in an oak at the far end of the glade. Demetrius remembered that the trees had spirits in them. As the spear quivered in the trunk, he wondered if he had committed an egregious error. But the elves laughed and went on with their games.

"You don't know your own strength," they teased him.

"This spear was wondrously light," he replied.

"It is made of wood like any human spear, but improved with elf magic," a young female said.

Ariella was next. She looked nervous since all the elves were watching her even as they pretended to care about nothing but their amusements. She tossed the spear once high in the air, testing its weight. Three leaping steps, and at the end of the third one, she released the spear.

An audible murmur of approval hummed all around. The spear had struck the target. Not in the very center, but solidly enough.

Mara stepped up next. The strength of her scrawny-looking arms was impressive, judging by how far she drew the bow. The arrow zinged home and hit the target with a satisfying thwack, not far from the center.

"My father taught me to use the bow when I was a wee lass," Mara said with a smile of false humility.

"Well, ladies, the beast is all yours. I will stand back while you hunt," Demetrius remarked.

Nevertheless, he walked up to the unfortunate tree he had hit, dug his spear out, and tried a few more throws, until finally his good aim returned and he was able to hit the target three times in a row.

A silvery sound echoed through the glade, the trumpeting of horns summoning them to the hunt. Two gorgeously attired elves rode forth, playing the instruments. Small metallic discs that hung from their hunting coats made beautiful chiming sounds in rhythm to their horses' trot.

"I heard these chimes when we first encountered them," Demetrius said.

Ariella nodded, looking at the two heralds' attire in fascination. "Perhaps that's why they call it the Ringing Woods."

Horses were led up to the company by young elves, and they all mounted. Demetrius was once again riding Mock, who looked well rested and content. Ariella mounted Destiny. Mara was given an elven steed. She looked beautiful in her red-haired opulence and her new elven attire, but she did nothing to stir Demetrius' heart.

Ariella, on the other hand, still wearing the same travel clothes, looked like the loveliest woman he had ever seen. Her walk may be about as smooth as that of a drunken sailor, albeit he still found it endearing, but her posture radiated grace as she rode. A stray lock of hair whipped across her forehead, and she brushed it away and smiled, suddenly noticing Demetrius' eyes on her.

"Come, dear guests, you shall ride by my side," Larkos beckoned.

He did not use a saddle nor even reins for his magical elven steed, but he rode with fluid perfection.

The riders streamed into the forest, Larkos in front, closely followed by Demetrius, Mara, and Ariella.

Mara looked resolute. Ariella seemed to be enjoying the day. Demetrius himself could not help but feel his spirits lift as he rode on, his face caressed by the passing winds. At the same time, he knew he could not let his guard down. A quiet but persistent inner voice warned him of some hidden peril.

The heralds were nowhere to be seen, but their chimes jingled here and there, intermingling with the varied forest sounds.

"The animal is likely to hear our approach, is it not?" Demetrius asked the king.

"Oh yes," Larkos replied in his airy way.

"Then why do the heralds make so much noise?"

"That way the beast can find us," Larkos explained as if it were the most obvious thing in the world.

Ariella exclaimed, "It wants to be hunted?"

"Of course," Larkos stated, "Otherwise we would never be able to find it. The Beolfia is stealthier than we shall ever be. But it enjoys the sport, so once in a while it allows us to catch up to it."

This left Demetrius puzzled. "Is there only one Beolfia?" he asked.

"In this forest, there is only one," Larkos replied. "They're very solitary."

Demetrius considered the implications of this. If there was only one Beolfia, then the elves should have no desire to kill it. Perhaps the attempt was what mattered.

His thought was interrupted, when Larkos cried, "Be ready! It approaches."

Just thirty feet onward, something luminescent broke through the greenery. It looked like a fleet creature streaking down from somewhere in the branches. It had moved so quickly that Demetrius could not even discern its shape or color; it piqued his curiosity.

"It has let itself be seen," Larkos whispered excitedly. "I think it will let us approach it."

They urged the horses on, heading in the direction where the beast last appeared.

Demetrius' eye was caught by sudden movement on his left: the creature was running alongside their cavalcade, as if mocking them.

The elves saw it too. They wheeled around, but too late – it was already weaving through the trees away from its pursuers. Even now, it moved so fast that Demetrius could hardly tell what it looked like. It was mostly grey, but some parts of it were colorful, and sleek as a panther.

In the blink of an eye, it disappeared from view. The elf king slowed his horse to a walk.

"It is here," he whispered. "Be careful."

The elves looked tense.

A rush of air made Demetrius look left, and then for the first time he clearly saw the creature – leaping directly at him. Time seemed to slow down, even as his heartbeat sped up.

The creature's silver eyes, long fangs and feline head were coming towards him. Its neck was encircled in a wreath of feathers that grew out of its body like a lion's mane. This feathery garland was iridescent, hypnotising.

Demetrius ducked, and his horse bounded forward, taking him out of harm's way. The Beolfia touched down only to spring away, but then looked back, daring him to follow.

Demetrius was about to hurl his spear. He was sure of his aim. It was one of those moments when the hunter gauges his distance and his strength perfectly and in some fatalistic way knows he cannot miss. He looked into the Beolfia's eyes.

Suddenly, he hesitated. An instinct told him that this creature was stronger than him. He may be able to wound it with his spear, but something unimaginably terrible awaited if he did so. Not only that, but he could sense its intelligence, its sensitivity, and he could tell it too was weighing its options against him.

He realized with unmistakable clarity that he did not want to hurt this beast, and the elves be damned. It was the same with hunting deer. He hated being the one to bring them down. And he was a free man now, not a slave. He could do as he pleased. If the elves were offended by his refusal to hunt, he would deal with them later.

Demetrius felt a sudden surge of relief as the creature looked away from him. At that moment, one of the young elves leapt from his saddle onto its back.

The two collapsed in a rolling heap. At first it seemed inconceivable that the elf could survive a barehanded tussle with this lightning-quick creature.

The young challenger was barely hanging on as the Beolfia lunged and weaved, trying to shake him free. Then the elf sprang away, and with daredevil courage, threw himself at the beast again, trying to bring it down. Instead, the Beolfia struck him with its paw and sent him flying into the nearest tree. The elves gasped – only to see their comrade hooking his legs around a bough as he flew through the air, then, like a practiced acrobat, swinging onto another branch and jumping neatly to the ground.

The Beolfia was now surrounded by a circle of elves, but it was obvious that although the creature looked cornered, it could break free at any moment. It seemed to be daring anyone to challenge it. The lion's tail whipped wildly back and forth. The silver eyes glared brazenly.

Across the circle from Demetrius, Mara aimed her bow. He wanted to shout a warning to her, but it was too late. She released the arrow. The bowstring twanged, and the elves froze in anticipation.

Moving with impossible speed, the Beolfia swatted the arrow aside with one of its paws. Then, with a roar that froze the blood in their veins, it rushed around the circle, and finally, stopping again in the middle, locked eyes with Mara.

The girl looked back, transfixed. A sudden pulse shook the forest, as if some invisible bolt of energy surged from the Beolfia straight towards Mara. She uttered a weak cry and fell back in a faint. The elf who rode beside her caught her before she slipped completely from the saddle, and Ariella hastened to dismount and lower her gently to the ground.

Another elf now challenged the Beolfia, but Demetrius ignored the scene of the hunt as he too jumped from his saddle and made his way towards his fallen companion.

Ariella was sitting on the ground as she cradled Mara's limp body. She looked up, distraught, as Demetrius approached.

Mara groaned feebly. Her eyes opened, and she sat up, assisted by Ariella.

"I wish it was only a dream," Mara whispered.

She seemed to be looking into the depths of some unfathomable horror.

"Mara! Are you all right?" Ariella cried.

Mara turned to her, and her lips stretched into a sad smile.

"I do not know if I was ever right," she murmured, "I lied

about my father teaching me to use a bow. It was a lover of mine, an archer of the king. He taught me, taught me a lot of things, and then left me, he did. Me and the baby."

"The baby?" Ariella exclaimed. "Where is your baby now?"

"It is better not to talk of it," Mara whispered. She suddenly began to sing, a sad, slow, dirge:

Among the meadows of sweet reverie
She wanders for eternity.

Ariella looked over at Demetrius as if beseeching him for help. A few feet away from them, the beast wrestled with Larkos.

"But who are you, gentle lady?" Mara asked, interrupting her own song and looking up at Ariella. "You, who are too kind to me?"

"Mara, you know me!"

But the girl only shook her head.

"Mara, if this is one of your tricks, I swear I'll kill you!" Ariella cried in a sudden rage.

Demetrius kneeled down beside them and put his hands on Ariella's shoulders trying to contain her anxiety.

Mara looked hard at Ariella, then burst into tears.

"I know you not," she sobbed, "Except... I remember you threatened to kill me before, but you never did. It's bad form to go back on one's promises."

"I'm sorry I threatened to kill you," Ariella said. Tears were welling up in her eyes too.

One of the elves approached them softly, and Demetrius recognized him from the spear throwing contest earlier. Like all the elves, he was lean and beautiful. His hair was the color of rose gold.

"She has been struck by the Beolfia," he said softly, "her mind is now lost."

"How do you mean?" Demetrius asked. "Does the Beolfia have such power?"

"Alas, yes," replied the elf. "Those who dare challenge the

Beast but have not tamed the beast within themselves, fall prey to its curse of madness."

Meanwhile, the hunt was unfolding before them like a scene from a dream, or a nightmare. The Beolfia was becoming vicious as it rolled on the ground, growling and striving to rid itself of Larkos. But the elf king would not release his grip, though the creature clawed at him. With his supernatural nimbleness, he dodged its deadly swipes every time, while still retaining his hold.

The beast stood up despite Larkos' efforts to pin it to the ground, and shook its body furiously from side to side. Still, the elf king did not relent. The creature growled, but stilled itself for a moment. It was at that moment that Larkos released his hold on the Beolfia and leapt down to the ground, facing the monster. His hands were out in a defensive stance, but he did not move. He was beautiful to behold. An elf's face is so much like a human's, but filled with more wisdom and beauty than a mortal could ever possess. Larkos looked knowingly at the beast as if trying to discern its secrets with his powerful mind. He did not have that strange radiance around him as he did the previous night, but there was an almost palpable sense of power about the way he stood, so sure of himself, yet not arrogant.

The looked into each other's eyes, two kings of the forest. At that moment, they appeared to be equals.

Another roar escaped the creature's frightening jaws. Larkos did not move. Then, without warning, the Beolfia sprang away, leaping clear over the heads of the mounted elves, and disappeared into the forest.

Larkos grinned, breathing heavily as he watched it go.

The elves lowered their spears, saluting him.

At this moment, Ariella stepped forward into the circle. Demetrius followed her and stood beside her, ready to defend her if it came to that. He sensed the fury building up within the warrior maiden.

"You look proud of yourself, Larkos," Ariella shouted. She pointed down to the ground, where Mara sat. "You think this is something to be proud of? Why have you done this to her?"

"I have not done it," Larkos replied, not raising his voice. "It was the will of the Beolfia."

"You never told us this could happen, that it could wreak insanity upon our minds."

"If I had told you, would you have come?" he retorted. "This hunt has been performed by our people for many hundreds of years. It must be done, and all our guests must do it too."

"But why?" Ariella's voice grew softer.

"It is a test."

"What if we didn't wish to be tested?"

"Do not fall into that trap of seeing yourself and your companions as victims," Larkos replied, a sudden sternness in his voice. "No one forced you to fight the Beolfia. You," he addressed Demetrius, "chose not to attack at the last moment. It was a wise choice. You've won a small battle, though your war is still before you. As for this poor child, she wanted to confront it head on. She has chosen her own fate."

Ariella had no reply for this. Demetrius could not decide whether Larkos truly meant those words, whether in his own way he was right.

"And I am sorry she failed," the elf king added.

CHAPTER 9

By the time the cavalcade returned for dinner, it was nearing dusk. They took a circuitous route back, riding for hours, it seemed. Ariella wondered whether Larkos was possibly doing it for her benefit, to give her temper a chance to cool. Perhaps it worked, for now she was tired and no longer in such a combative mood.

It seemed they were back at the same glade, but they had meandered along so many forest paths that Ariella had lost all sense of direction, and it was very likely a completely different place. All the trees looked altered in the evening light. The small shelters, similar to the ones in which they had spent the night, stood in the same circular formation, but now there seemed to be a few more of them than before.

There was also a long table set underneath a canopy of woven branches with fireflies hovering around them.

The tree choir sang harmoniously. Unlike the previous night, when the tree spirits had seemed intent on scaring the travelers out of their wits, they now sounded tame and soothing. Ariella would have been overwhelmed by the wonder of it all if her companion had not just been rendered insane. She suddenly wished she was back in Leduryon by her own fireplace, surrounded by yawning swifthounds.

Mara had ridden all the way in dour silence interspersed with nonsensical utterings. Now, the three of them were separated as the elves led them into different cabins to rest before dinner.

Ariella collapsed onto the bed as soon as she entered the cabin. She napped for what felt like an hour. When she awoke, she realized that clothes had been prepared for her and were laid out on a small table by her bedside. It was already dark, and she noticed the fabric shimmering in the moonlight as though it were made of tiny gems.

When she was dressed and ready to step out of her cabin, she opened the door to reveal a feast laid out on the long table beneath the firefly-lighted canopy. Elves were arriving to take their seats, while Larkos already lounged gracefully at the midpoint of the table. Demetrius sat beside him, and they were discussing something, though Ariella was too far away to hear them.

They saw Ariella, and both froze where they sat. She thought it was rather funny that both man and elf were so stunned by her appearance. The attire she had been given must have had something to do with it. It was a long, flowing dress, lighter than silk and glittering with many tiny specs that were woven into it by some incredible magic or artistry. The bodice clung to her torso perfectly, outlining the curve of her breasts, while the skirt billowed in wild patterns as the wind played with its translucent layers.

At this moment, Mara exited her cabin, where she too had been resting. Her eyes were still wild and otherworldly, as they had become after her encounter with the Beolfia. In spite of this, Ariella approached her, wanting so badly to try to break through the barrier of her madness.

"Mara, are you feeling better?" she asked.

"No, no," Mara replied sadly, "I'll never feel better."

Ariella reached out to clasp her shoulders, but Mara swerved away and ran to the edge of the clearing. Ariella feared she would run off into the woods, but instead Mara sat down underneath a tree, her legs folded and resting on the ground.

The tree spirit had already sprung to life and was dancing before her. For a long while she looked up at it. Ariella wondered whether the shifting form of the tree spirit was something akin to what Mara's madness would look like if it had a shape.

"Do you mind if I sit here and talk to you?" Mara asked the tree spirit.

It made the same musical sounds as usual, and she seemed to take it as a yes.

Ariella took a deep breath. Evidently this madness was going to be long-lasting, if not permanent. She decided to join the revellers instead, for it looked like everyone was assembled for the feast.

It did not have the rowdy and wild character of a human celebration. Humans often competed, trying to talk the loudest, look the most beautiful, or drink the most wine. Here, everyone simply was. If they did need to prove themselves, it must have been in subtle ways that Ariella could not comprehend.

Larkos silently indicated to her a place beside him. He stood up and bowed to her as she took her seat. Not to be outdone in courtesy, Demetrius did likewise.

"What were you talking about?" Ariella asked them as Larkos poured her a goblet full of wine.

The cakes they were eating looked delicious, and Ariella reached for one. Everyone around her was using their hands, so she did not stand on ceremony.

"The hunt," Larkos said cryptically.

Ariella took a bite of the cake and discovered she had drifted away to the heavenly realms. It was sweet and chewy, and filled with the taste and scent of the most delicious flowers.

"I was just wondering," Demetrius explained, "if one who does not challenge the Beolfia is completely safe from it."

"Indeed that is so," said Larkos, "though one is still not safe from oneself."

"Too true," Demetrius remarked.

Larkos turned to Ariella, looking intently into her eyes.

"You never intended to hunt the beast," he stated more as a fact than a question.

Ariella shrugged. "No. I didn't want to. Though now that I see your intention was never to kill it, I almost regret it. I wonder how I would have fared."

The guests at the table were mostly elves, but there were others who could only have been thought of as oddities. A half-man-half-boar lounged on the far side, devouring everything within reach, food remnants smeared all over its snout. Closer to the center sat an ethereally beautiful woman with languid blue eyes, long wheat blond hair stretching so far back that it disappeared into the tree branches, where it moved and braided itself like a living thing, combed by unseen creatures. There was also a human warrior, sitting further off, who remained perfectly silent, ever-present tears streaming down his face. He did not eat, but only drank the wine.

"They have either strayed into our forest or come here out of desire to find us," Larkos explained, guessing her thoughts before she had a chance to speak them. "We do not force anyone to stay."

"Is Mara to become just one more addition to this strange gathering?" Ariella blurted out. "Are they all here to amuse you?"

The king looked at her gravely, then put a hand to his chest.

"Ariella, you already wound my heart with your beauty. I pray you do not hurt me further with your accusations of callousness."

It was then that she saw him as a male for the first time. He had seemed a creature far above them in knowledge and power, too mystical to have an interest in love and its fatuous games. But now she beheld the fire in his eyes. His features were perfect, so perfect that it made it obvious he was not human. Such a beautiful face would be considered too feminine and laughed at by her fellow warriors in Dezearre, but Ariella was secretly partial to it.

"Be merciful," he entreated, his elfish smile a beguiling

mixture of sensuality and mystery.

Ariella struggled to maintain a stern expression, but the right corner of her lips escaped her control and curled upwards. In the next instant, she was furious with herself for giving in to his charm. She felt her face flush. In order to conceal her conflicting emotions, she downed a whole goblet of wine, hiding behind it, if only for a moment.

She suddenly remembered that the king could read people's hearts and minds. He probably already knew much more about her than she cared to reveal, and there was nothing she could do about it.

"What will happen to Mara?" Ariella asked, putting her goblet down.

"She will stay here. In her state, the outside world is too dangerous a place for her. Do not look so gloomy, my dear, she may yet recover. And if she does, she will be free to leave our forest. I know humans believe we hold everyone here by force, but truly, that is not our way."

"Then do you think there is a chance she will regain her clarity of mind?" Ariella asked.

"Of course. And I will try to help."

Another promise made by a man, or at least a man-like creature. Ariella did not know whether to believe a word he said.

"I know, I may have omitted some facts before, but I hope you have faith in me," Larkos replied to her thoughts once again.

Ariella had to admit that his grey eyes were beautiful and hypnotic, set in a flawless face. He had the appeal of mystery on his side. She was sure that as mere human visitors they had seen only a fraction of the elves' true existence. But then again, that mystery held some frightening secrets, as she had seen this day.

"Faith is not something I'm very good at," she replied. "If I ever see Mara again, if she is of sound mind, then we may resume talking on… this subject."

Larkos leaned closer to her. "I will remember your words

and treasure them."

Ariella felt her whole body ignite with his closeness. She could not understand whether it was some elfish magic, or simply the allure of his beauty that affected her.

"May I ask for one favor?" Larkos asked.

"I don't know," Ariella teased, "Tell me what it is first."

On the one hand, she could not believe herself. On the other hand, she knew herself well enough to know that wine combined with a handsome man made her outrageously flirtatious.

"Could you give me a small gift ere you depart?" he asked.

For a brief moment, she looked over at Demetrius and noted that he was conspicuously not looking in their direction.

"What gift would that be?" Ariella suddenly felt butterflies in her stomach.

"Only the band you use to tie your hair."

She felt both relieved and disappointed.

"Of course," she said, "it is a very small gift for such a gracious host."

She removed the tie from her hair, which now flowed loose across her shoulders.

At the closing of the feast, the elves led their guests each to their own cabin as before. Ariella noted where Mara and Demetrius were being taken as she herself was shown into the same cabin where she had rested after the hunt.

She sat down on the flowery bed and tried to think. Too much had happened that day, and she wanted to unravel her tangled emotions.

It was the second night in a row she was to spend alone, without Demetrius. Ariella could not believe how quickly she had become accustomed to sleeping with her arm draped over him, feeling the steadiness of his breath. She thought that perhaps she understood now how married couples feel, the security and the warmth of the other person always beside them.

A soft laugh escaped her lips: she suddenly recognized the ridiculousness of comparing her brief nightly encounters with a secretive stranger to full-fledged marriage.

In the next instant, she heard a knock at the door of her cabin. The door opened, for whoever was without did not have the patience to wait for a reply and there was no lock. For a brief second, she felt both the fear and the thrill of the possibility that it was Larkos, but then she recognized the strong, muscular shape silhouetted against the moonlight and the silvery light of the trees, and her heart hammered faster against her ribcage.

"What's so funny?" Demetrius asked.

"I am simply laughing because of that old saying that the flesh is weak and the spirit is even weaker."

"That's funny?" he asked, seemingly unconvinced, though she suspected that he knew how that saying applied in this instance. "Well, after a day like today, I'm glad that something is funny."

"So am I," Ariella agreed.

"I just wanted to... see you," he said.

"And to make sure Larkos was not prowling around my cabin?" Her tone was jocular, but she longed to know the answer.

In the darkness, she saw his chest straining, lifting with a sigh.

"Ariella, even if I feel jealous, I have no right. But I could see that he's taken with you."

He came closer.

"I wanted to see you too," Ariella admitted. "And I understand... or at least I have the feeling that you cannot make me any promises about the future."

"That much is true," he agreed. "I can make no promise about what the future holds, for my fate has never been my own. But at the very least, we did have an agreement about three nights of our voyage. And now, tonight, I am yours."

The night air was still and filled with their unexpressed longing, but those words made her forget her own sadness about Mara and her yearning to know Demetrius' unspoken, secret sorrow.

She stood up from the bed and her lips were on his. He responded to her kiss just as passionately as she had lunged at him.

His fingers found the laces of her dress, tugging at them with impatient urgency. Feeling the dress loose, she wriggled out of it, still locked in his embrace, still kissing his warm lips, and the dress slid off her body like a smoothly flowing rivulet.

Demetrius barely broke away from her to remove his own clothing, the bandage wrapped around his chest and over one shoulder now his only covering, and as he pulled her down towards him, they floated on the airy bed. Ariella sighed, reveling in the feeling of her entire body aligned perfectly with his from head to foot, the feel of his skin, and the heavy yet comforting weight of him. Simply pressing him against her felt heavenly.

His stubble tickled her face as he kissed her cheek, then her temple and her ear. A playful bite on her earlobe made her squirm with lust. Every single touch awakened new desires she didn't even know she had: his fingernails tickling feather-light down her back, his lips kissing all the way down her arm and exploring the tender skin in the fold of her elbow, his tongue stimulating the sensitive, silky skin of her thighs.

As his hair tickled her legs, she looked down at him in this position, feeling once again like a queen looking down upon her slave. But this time, he was far from being one. This time, for the first time ever, they were both free to do as they wished, and he chose to please himself by pleasing her.

She uttered a soft cry when his tongue first touched the soft flower between her thighs. Demetrius looked up at her with a grin, evidently proud of the effect he was having already. His eyes reflecting the moonlight, the angles of his face looked even more beautiful, his cheekbones highlighted by silver light and shadow. He bent to his enjoyable task, two stray locks of hair hanging down his forehead and moving with his rhythm. She gathered the dark waves of his hair to help him easily access the heart of her pleasure, but left the two stray locks that accented his face.

She gasped, feeling the warmth of his tongue pressing inside her. She was sweating now, writhing in a frenzy of passion. Just when she thought it could not be more powerful, she was captured and sucked intensely by his relentless mouth. She felt the roughness of his stubble on her most sensitive parts, and it was an unbearable pleasure, its rough surface stoking the fire of her easily aroused organ. This exciting torment could only be quelled in a climax, but Demetrius would not let her reach it so soon.

He released some of the pressure, then commenced licking her with long, intense strokes. Brief bursts of sensation raced up her spine and made her moan, but they were not enough to bring the rapture to its peak.

Using the grip she had on his hair, she gently pulled his head down, desperate for him to exert a stronger pressure, to rub his rough stubble more forcefully across her exposed skin.

"My lady is impatient?" he asked, raising his head and smiling wickedly.

She nodded, panting.

"Then I shall not keep you waiting."

His mouth knew its task well. She could feel he was no longer teasing now but stirring up her passion, striving to help her reach the heights of pleasure.

His tongue slid deeper into her, then his lips surrounded her mound, squeezing the pleasurable sensation out, letting it spill over the rest of her body. Before she realized it, the waves savagely tore her away from all control, surging down her legs and up her torso... she shuddered as the energy coursed through her again and again.

When it subsided, she opened her eyes, listening to the mad thrashing of her own heartbeat and seeing her surroundings as if for the first time. Demetrius was at her side, kissing her gently and soothingly, but the gentleness soon built up to more passion. Not only passion, but also affection. She sensed it in the way he hugged her close to him, nuzzled her neck, and kissed her face, each imprint of his lips like a secret whisper of adoration. There was no denying it: she was not just enjoying the closeness of his body either. They had been through so many trials together, and it made them more than just casual companions.

She wrapped her legs tightly around him, enclosing him in a trap from which he obviously had no desire to escape. His breath held the delicious scent of elven wine. Ariella realized she was moaning softly as he kissed the palm of her hand and licked her arm. He adored her entire body, not just the usual parts that are associated with pleasure and lust. Even her armpit, which she had never considered the most beautiful body part, was fair game for his roving tongue. But when he did focus his attention on the more sensual areas of her breasts, the feeling was so intense it nearly sent her over the edge again. His lips closed around the darker skin of her nipple, and his tongue teased her hardening tip with gentle touches. Then all at once, he sucked greedily at her breast's tiny mound, making her cry out. The intensity of it shot through her body like the strongest of liquors, and the sudden arousal she felt in her sex made her dig her fingernails into his back. She craved more.

He released her left breast, sending a light breath across her moist skin that chilled her and aroused her.

"Are you ready for me, my love?" he asked.

For a moment, she was stunned by the word 'love' and wondered whether he truly felt that emotion. Of course, it was just a word. He could have been just carried away by the throes of passion. He was gazing into her eyes, his face even more handsome than ever, eyes smouldering.

She suddenly realized that she had forgotten to answer his question. She bit her lip and uttered a small laugh.

"Yes," she said, "more than ready."

"Oh, Ariella," he groaned as he began to enter her.

He looked completely intoxicated with her body. It made her feel desirable and so connected to him as he filled her. She had become accustomed to his size. It was the most pleasurable feeling now, allowing him so fully inside, being one with him, his heat melding with hers until they were the same.

His powerful muscles tensed with the rhythm of his motion. Ariella wanted to release the building tension in a flurry of screams, but she felt it would somehow be wrong in the elf sanctuary, seeing how thin the walls of the cabin were… His thrusts came faster and stronger. Oh, it was too much… and yet just perfect.

The need to hold in her screams of pleasure made the passion she felt even more intense.

Her hands gripped his back, urging him on, scratching him with her nails. Her legs wrapped around him to bring him even closer, to connect with him at every possible part of her body. Before she knew it, her heartbeat was pounding madly, and the first flood of pleasure carried her off on its mad current.

He cried her name as his face took on a beautifully savage look, and his muscular body convulsed in her arms. The warmth of his juices flowed into her belly, filling it with one last dose of pleasure.

As their breathing returned to normal, he still remained inside her. They stayed like this for a while, deeply and gently kissing.

Although satisfied for the moment, Ariella suddenly knew she was craving more.

"Again?" she asked.

"If my lady wishes," he replied.

"If you wish it too," she insisted.

His smouldering eyes scorched her.

"I've never wanted anything this badly," he said.

Ariella knew she would never forget this night.

He took her to new heights of pleasure again and again. She had never been so aroused, so filled to the brim and still craving more. At last, they collapsed, completely exhausted in each other's arms.

Sweet, languorous kisses… She was too tired and too satisfied for anything more strenuous, but these kisses were perfect, and it seemed Demetrius didn't want to part from her lips either.

"You are impossible to resist," he said, "You must have

hordes of admirers back in Dezearre."

"Oh, hardly," she scoffed.

"I don't believe that," Demetrius stated.

Was he trying to find out whether she was engaged back in her homeland? Well, if he could have his secrets, so could she. If he did not ask directly, she would not answer. She was too young when her parents died, and they had not yet selected a match for her. Ariella herself was in no rush to make such a momentous decision.

If Demetrius knew that she was not spoken for, what would he do? No, she was not ready to have a conversation like that. Besides, she didn't know whether there was someone waiting for him, didn't want to know.

A couple of minutes later, his breathing became deep and steady. He was already asleep.

Ariella smirked. Like most men, he was claimed by sleep so quickly after lovemaking. But, in many ways, he was not like most men.

She was struck by the thought that she had never had such a skillful, passionate and caring lover, and probably never would again. It was too much to think about, and she tried not to give in to despair. Even when she made it safely back home, nothing would be the same again.

As the years passed after her parents' death, she had come to believe that life was too fleeting and too uncertain a thing not to be enjoyed to the fullest. That was why she often spent nights drinking to excess or bedding strange men that suited her fancy. After all, each night could be her last, for nothing was solid in life, and no promise of the future could remain unbroken.

But this time, she had wanted Demetrius so badly, it was not merely the usual philosophy of taking what you can while you can. It was an unquenchable longing for his presence, his touch.

She only hoped that she had not gone too far, that she would not yearn for him while lying alone in her bed back in her castle on long winter nights.

CHAPTER 10

Waking up in the elf cabin was so pleasant that Demetrius forgot all his worries. Mornings were usually his least favorite time; it was when doubts and fears crept unbidden into his mind, and he was not yet awake enough to shake them off. This morning was different.

The air was fresh and carried with it flower and pine smells from the forest. Demetrius lay next to the woman who had become, by strange turns of events, his lover. She seemed half-awake as she turned towards him and kissed his lips as if it were the most habitual action in the world for her.

When they emerged from the tent, they found some of the younger elves up to their old games just like the day before. This time, Demetrius showed off his improved spear throwing, but the elves still laughed at him, poking fun at his embarrassing misses the previous morning. He laughed with them.

When they grew tired of their exercises, the elves simply collapsed onto the fresh grass, one after the other and lay there, resting. Ariella shrugged, and followed their example, laughing giddily. Demetrius lay down beside her and without really thinking about why he did it, took her hand as they lay in the grass. They both looked up at the clear sky, framed by towering trees that seemed to rush upward into its depths.

Demetrius would have given so much just to be able to live out the rest of his life here. He did not say much, and neither did Ariella. Their eyes met, and they both knew they needed no words, both equally enjoying the day and still glowing from their tryst of the previous night.

It was at that moment that for some strange reason, Demetrius longed to tell Ariella his secrets, why he could make no promise about the future. It would of course completely destroy the wonderful moment they were sharing, but at least his conscience would be clear. Would she reject him? Or perhaps just pity him?

If he were stronger, he certainly would have told her. But he admitted his weakness and pushed those thoughts aside, choosing to stay in the present moment instead. Of course, he knew their idyllic time was coming to an end.

"What are you thinking about now?" she asked.

Damn, but she was too quick. She could see right through him.

"You don't want to know," Demetrius replied.

"Then we are probably thinking the same thing," she said.

Of course, this day could not go on forever. When Demetrius saw Larkos approaching them, he knew it was time to leave. They had already stayed too long.

Larkos smiled with a hint of sadness, as if he too had guessed that they were of a mind to leave.

Ariella looked most sad of all, for despite her anger over Mara's fate, she had quickly grown accustomed to the elf forest. She seemed perfectly at home there. Demetrius wondered how much of it had to do with Larkos, what feelings Ariella truly had for the elf king. Of course, he had no right to ask her that. The way she looked at Larkos, the way her eyes lit up with fascination… perhaps it was nothing more than that. And Larkos was not the one she had held all night, writhing in his arms, kissing, stroking…

Larkos and the others saw them off as they saddled their horses and said their final farewells. There was no sign of

Mara, and Demetrius noticed that Ariella was looking about to try and spot her, but in vain.

"I hope you will see your friend again, soon," Larkos said. His face gave nothing away. "And know that you're always welcome here if ever again you need our help."

Ariella smiled. "You're welcome in my castle too."

"And in mine," Demetrius added. "We owe you our lives."

Larkos nodded in thanks. Demetrius could tell that his feelings ran deep, but were contained.

"Ride down this path, always keeping north-west, and you will soon find your way to Dezearre."

Although she had only traveled a day and a night with them, they felt Mara's absence.

By nightfall, they were out of the Ringing Woods and into the Aspen Forest. It was just a forest like many others, not inhabited by elves or magical tree spirits. Occasionally a deer crossed their path and sprang away as silently as it had come.

They were on the territory of Dezearre. Everything was drier here, more fragile. The lushness of Chaldea was replaced by smaller, thinner trees. Here, the coming autumn would bring a long season of frigid winds, ice, and snow. Soon Demetrius would have to head south to his homeland.

The shadows of twilight were falling upon the forest when the riders saw a larger than usual clearing up ahead. Emerging from between the trees, they realized it was a patch of farm land.

An ancient, weather-beaten house stood on the side of the road, with a scattering of barns beyond it. The house looked like it had been made of nothing but straw and mud or perhaps dung, with a sparse timber frame to hold it up.

"Perhaps this should be our resting place for the night?" Demetrius queried. "It's getting dark. Though if we journey on, we may find slightly more graceful lodgings."

"This or another one, what does it matter," Ariella replied wearily. "After the elven forest, any human-made building will seem drab in comparison."

For an instant Demetrius felt the acidic bite of jealousy, eating away at the edges of his mind. He could not help recalling the interest Ariella showed in the elf king, the way she reacted to his attention. It had not all been one-sided. Of course, she was free in her affections, and he wanted her to be happy.

"You never know," he countered lightly, "some human dwellings may surprise you."

She smiled as they rode on. As long as that smile beamed its light on him, all his other concerns dissipated like morning mist.

The farmer came out, bearing a small torch. He was an old and haggard man, a match for his house. His head was bound with a blue handkerchief, and a few grey strands poked out from beneath the fabric. The sweat of the day's work still glistened on his face. He narrowed his eyes suspiciously, the wrinkles around his eyes born of squinting in the sun deepening, but perhaps seeing that the riders were not heavily armed and not numerous, he assumed a more gracious air.

He bid the travelers good evening and bowed respectfully.

"Good evening," Demetrius replied, "We seek shelter."

"If you would oblige us, we shall repay you most generously," Ariella added.

The farmer bowed again, looking discomfited.

"Good sir, good lady, I can offer you food and wine. As for shelter, there are but the humblest of beds in my house… as you can see, time has not been kind to it. My mother sleeps on top of the stove, and my son and me share the other bed. But it is yours, such as it is."

"No, no, we couldn't take your bed," Ariella contended. "Where would you sleep?"

"My son and me, we can be plenty comfortable in the stable."

"Then that's where Lady Ariella and I will sleep," Demetrius said.

The farmer did not dare object any further. The riders dismounted, and the old man took the horses' reins, insisting that he would stable their mounts, while they should go in and warm themselves.

They entered the house. It was strangely quiet, with only the old woman who was evidently the farmer's mother, dozing on top of the massive brick stove, the only well-built structure in this squalid dwelling.

Demetrius and Ariella sat down on a bench at the small square table. The owner of the house joined them soon after stabling the horses and began to fuss about the small space preparing supper.

"You have ridden from afar?" he asked looking at them over his shoulder as he stirred the soup.

"Yes, from Chaldea," Demetrius replied. "I am returning home to Sylcadia."

"And you, my lady? If I am not mistaken, you are from these parts."

"I am," Ariella replied. "My name is Ariella, Baroness of Leduryon."

"And you, good sir? What shall I call you?"

"Demetrius, Baron of Athelis."

"You are both welcome. I'm Meryall Remfrey. Call me Meryall. My son is herding the cattle on the far pasture, but he will be home soon, and we shall all have supper. My son used to serve at the royal palace in Sylcadia, by the way. His mother was from there, though now she walks the pastures of the Blessed Lands. Now that she is gone to her rest, he lives with me."

Demetrius tried to hide his worry, but the mention of the royal palace sent a shiver down his spine. Of course it had been so many years ago, and he had been but a skinny youth then. Surely, the farmer's son would not be able to recognize him.

"You must have passed through good swathe of forest to get here," Remfrey commented.

"Oh yes," they replied.

"To go around the elf lands, I mean," he added.

"Indeed," Ariella confirmed politely.

Demetrius winked conspirationally. He believed it was best not to reveal their journey through the elf lands. Farm folk could be superstitious and consider it bad luck to receive visitors who had so recently colluded with the dangerous and occult powers of the elves.

The little house slowly filled with the aroma of beef and herbs. Just as they prepared to feast on the steaming bowls of soup placed before them, the door squeaked open and a young man of thirty or so appeared. He had a healthy, sun-kissed look, invigorated rather than exhausted by his work.

Demetrius and Ariella rose up from the table to meet the new arrival.

"At last!" Meryall exclaimed, "This is my son, Joce."

The young man smiled cordially at the visitors, but when he came closer and was about to address Demetrius, his smile faded, and his face took on an expression of utter astonishment.

For a moment, everyone was silent. Demetrius held his breath. He had met Joce before, that was certain. The lad had been a servant in the royal palace. But Demetrius still did not truly think Joce would recognize him... that is, until he said his name.

"Is it really you, Prince Lennell?" the young man uttered.

Demetrius sighed with a feeling akin to relief. At least he did not have to wonder anymore.

"Yes, it's me, Joce. You worked in the palace kitchen, did you not?"

The man nodded. Without saying another word, he kneeled on the sod floor, Demetrius watching him uncomfortably. Everyone else stared, not knowing what to say.

"Please, Joce, no need for this," he pleaded, "It's been a while since anyone bowed or kneeled before me."

"Your highness," Joce said, standing up. "I am overjoyed to see you."

"Your highness?" Ariella turned to him, anger simmering in her tone. "You are a prince? Your name is Lennell?"

Demetrius felt like the earth had opened up to swallow

him. He wished it would do as much.

"I am sorry I didn't tell you sooner," he replied. "I am Lennell Demetrius Symond, Crown Prince of Sylcadia."

Ariella stood frozen in disbelief for a moment. The next instant, she simply strode out of the house, the shocked glances of the farmer and his nephew directed at her back.

"Excuse me one moment," Demetrius said to the stunned family.

He rushed out of the house and spotted Ariella walking hurriedly towards the fields. He ran to catch up with her.

His heart pounded, though not from running, and he inhaled ragged lungfuls of cold air that carried a smell of manure. His thoughts were so dismal it was dizzying. Now that Ariella knew that he was the crown prince of Sylcadia and not just some minor baron, she would probably know that he was engaged to Duchess Edoline. It had been a celebrated political alliance forged many years ago.

"Stop!" he cried. "Ariella, wait!"

She turned sharply to face him, and he recognized the combative expression her face would take on before a big fight.

"You are engaged!" she cried.

He finally caught up and they stood facing each other about three feet apart. He felt she might run away again if he came any closer.

"Yes, to a young woman whom I have known since we were children."

"Really? Do you enjoy twisting the knife in the wound?"

"No, you're not listening," Demetrius pleaded. "Duchess Edoline, she's like a sister to me, a childhood playmate. Our engagement was something that was done when I was still a child, as you well know; I had no hand in it!"

"Well, that is just fine. I care not if you are engaged to a duchess or a donkey. It is all the same to me."

"I can see very well how much you don't care," he scoffed.

Ariella spun away from him, hugging herself, head lowered.

"I'm sorry," she said in a hollow voice. "You're right, this is no one's business but your own. Ours was merely a chance encounter, and soon we will part ways."

"No, no," Demetrius took hold of her shoulders and gently turned her to face him. He wished he could discern and understand the myriad of emotions flitting across her eyes. "We're not strangers, Ariella, are we?"

She shook her head. Her mouth was so tantalizingly close, so inviting with its luscious contours. The color of her lips looked mauve in the darkness. He wanted nothing more than to kiss her, to make her forget their situation even if for a moment.

"At the very least we are friends," he said softly.

Before he knew it, she was holding him tightly, her head nestled on his shoulder. He held her close.

He had no notion of how long they stood there outside the farm house in the dark.

At last, Ariella said, "We should go in. We've interrupted our hosts' dinner."

"We will talk more about this later, all right?" Demetrius asked.

She nodded. He could see that she was being strong, but he had not realized until now just how deeply her feelings ran. Yet he did not allow himself to assume they were feelings of affection; it could have been simply anger at being deceived by someone she had trusted.

When they re-entered the house, the family, including Meryall's elderly mother, were seated on the crude benches around the table.

"You didn't tell me we had guests, Meryall!" the old woman exclaimed.

She looked so frail that it was a wonder she could sit upright.

"I'm sorry, ma," Meryall said. "I forgot, what with all the excitement of making soup."

"Grandmamma Magdelne, this is Lennell Demetrius, prince of Sylcadia," Joce said, eager to see her reaction.

"It's a great honor!" Magdelne replied. "And the young

lady?"

"Ariella, of Leduryon," Ariella beamed, looking instantly charmed by the grandmother.

"Why, that's not far from here," Grandmamma Magdelne said, "I used to deliver eggs to your grandfather. The old baron, may the stars guide his soul, wanted only the best eggs, and mine were the best."

"I must take after the old man," Ariella replied. "For fried eggs are one of my favorite things in the world. If you could have Joce deliver some of your fabulous eggs to me, I will give you a fair price."

"Oh but I'm too old to raise chickens now," the old woman protested, "Who would sleep on the stove if I was out in the barn all day?"

"I could do that!" Joce volunteered.

Everyone laughed. It seemed they were all eager to latch on to even the smallest shreds of humor to lighten the mood after what had happened. The soup tasted just as good as it smelled, and the hungry travelers devoured it in great gulps without standing on ceremony.

Demetrius felt a comforting warmth in his body and soul. Watching Ariella with her countrymen, he had a sense that she was a generous and just baroness. She probably cared for all her people with the same concern she had shown in trying to care for Mara.

"Did you travel through the elf lands?" Magdelne asked, putting a sudden stop to her family's chatter.

"Ma! What a thing to say!" Meryall admonished.

"It's all right," Demetrius replied. He looked over at Ariella, uncertain how to continue.

"We might as well tell them," Ariella said.

"We did travel through the elf lands," Demetrius confirmed.

"How did you make it out alive?" Joce wondered.

"I honestly think Ariella caught the eye of the elf king," Demetrius said half-jokingly. He winked at her, and she smiled back.

"My cousin ran off to the elf lands, you know." Magdelne's faded green eyes looked off into some distant landscapes of the past. "She was always wishing for a better life, wondering what lay beyond the forest. A beautiful lass she was, with long lustrous hair down to her knees. Have you seen her, I wonder?"

Demetrius thought of the woman whose hair disappeared into the forest at the elves' feast.

"We may have... though it is hard to say. Everything becomes transformed there."

"I had a feeling she was still alive, still there," Magdelne said wistfully.

"I heard no one can leave," Joce remarked, "and the ones that manage to escape are all mad as pickors."

"Such was the fate of our companion," Ariella murmured.

An uncomfortable silence filled the little house. It was the grandmother's voice that broke the ice again.

"When will you two be married then?" she asked cheerfully.

"Ma, will you ever stop poking your nose into people's business?" Meryall reprimanded.

"We are not..." Demetrius began, but did not know how to end the sentence.

"I know, dears, it takes time. I know," Magdlene reassured him, "Why, Meryall's father, my late husband, took two years to work up the courage to propose to me. And you would think he would be hardier, being a stout and brawny fellow as he was. No, when it comes down to the grind, it's the men who always sag like soggy deadwood."

"Grandmamma, you're scaring our guests," Joce said with a grin.

"Oh I'll stop now," she said, an unrepentant gleam in her eye. "Eat your soup, dears."

Despite Meryall's repeated offers of his bed, the guests decided to retire to the stable after dinner. Demetrius knew they needed to talk further in private, and he preferred the smell of hay to the close air of the house. Besides, he did not want to deprive his gracious hosts of their bed. He held a small lantern Meryall had given him to light their way.

"And you thought we would never see something as wonderful as the elves' forest," he said to Ariella as they climbed the ladder to the hayloft, "What are the elven dwellings compared to this hayloft? Nothing at all."

Ariella chuckled grudgingly. "If you're a horse, maybe."

They settled down in the hay, burying themselves in it to keep out the night chill. Ariella moved a few feet away from him.

"It's the wrong time of the month now," she said, "I wouldn't want to produce an illegitimate heir to your kingdom."

Her anger simmered in the small space.

"Grandmamma Magdlene brought up a good point though," he said casually. "We are a fitting couple. We look good together, you can't deny that. More than that, we feel good together. If you feel the same thing I feel, that is. What would you say if I asked my parents to break the engagement?"

There was a moment of hesitation before she replied, and Demetrius was almost sure she wanted to say yes. At last she replied, "That would be foolish. They would never go back on their word and risk unrest within your kingdom."

"I believe they could be persuaded in time," he insisted.

"And what shall we do in the meantime, create a whole litter of royal bastards?"

"Sounds like a fine activity to me," Demetrius said.

She snorted with disdain.

"I am sorry I didn't tell you before," he called out.

She was perfectly still, somewhere a few feet beyond him in the darkness. "Why didn't you?"

"I don't know... Maybe I didn't want you to know I was engaged, that I was the crown prince. I just wanted everything to be the way it was when we first met. That night was so magnificent."

"I'm truly amazed that you were able to hold on to your secret that long," she said, the same disdain in her voice.

Demetrius lay back in the hay, gazing at a sliver of black sky and a small flickering star visible through a large crack in the barn roof. Below, he could hear the horses, breathing softly.

"After so many years in Chaldea, I've become accustomed to keeping so much inside. It's no wonder I could not tell you about myself. It will take practice to re-learn to do that again, I suppose."

He heard the hay shifting nearby. As his eyes adjusted to the darkness, he saw her sitting up.

"Demetrius, I am sorry," she said, "Sometimes I forget all you have been through. So many years…"

"No, I am the one who is sorry," he insisted, "None of this was your doing."

"Wasn't it, though?"

"The first time we made love, it was my duty to entertain you. The second time, it was our duty to entertain Vidor's guests. As for the third time, I came to you because I was jealous of the elf king, and because I wanted your touch, I needed it. I can barely comprehend how I will be able to go on without seeing you every day. Please tell me you feel at least something for me?"

He listened intently for her answer as if his life depended on it.

"Yes, I do feel as if we've formed a bond," she said, her voice barely audible, "and you're right it was not my doing, nor yours. It simply happened before we became aware of it."

She did feel something! He released a breath that he had not even been aware of holding. But he knew she was still angry with him, understandably so.

"That is why I forgive you for not telling me the truth," she added at length.

His heart soared, but instantly sank like a stone at her next utterance.

"And that is why we must forget this ever happened."

He shouted before he could stop himself. "You can forget all this if you want, but I will not!"

In a burst of desperation, he suddenly found himself holding her hands and kneeling before her as she sat listlessly, strangely lacking in defiance. It was so unlike her. Then he saw the glistening tears streaming down her cheeks.

He reached for her, and his heart fluttered as if he were leaping over a deep chasm. He hoped she would let him hold her and comfort her.

She didn't pull away. Soon, her arms were intertwined around him. She clasped him to her chest with real warmth.

"We've grown too close. I only wish to spare us the pain," she said at last.

"Well, I don't," he said, all his rage subsiding as he carefully wiped away her tears with his hand, "I don't want to forget you, even if I could."

"What is the point of remembering?" she asked. "Tomorrow, we must part ways, you to your homeland, and I to mine."

"Have you forgotten the promise I gave you?" Demetrius said softly, looking into her tearful eyes, "As soon as I have brought news of my freedom to my kingdom, I will come back to you. That is, if you permit me?"

Finally, she looked up at him with something other than sadness. There was a spark of hope in her eyes, like a tiny but fiercely burning star in the night sky.

"No," she said, and he felt his heart crumpling in his chest, until the next words she spoke revived it. "Not unless you can somehow break your engagement."

"Then I will try," he affirmed.

"Even if it endangers your kingdom?"

"For you…" he began. He could hardly express how much he was willing to do for her. "The kingdom could go to hell for just one night with you. Imagine what I would do to keep you forever."

At least this produced an amused smile.

"Ariella, I want you!" he exclaimed. "There is no one I would rather hold in my arms."

"You did promise me three nights…" she admitted. "But you have already delivered on that promise."

This was more like the Ariella he knew. She definitely had a playful streak.

"I promised three nights and more," he argued.

She drew a deep breath, considering his offer coquettishly. "Oh very well, I will accept the 'more.'"

"What about time of the month?" he asked, breathless.

"I lied. I was angry with you. I think it is still safe."

Without another word, he kissed her with insatiable hunger. He felt her excitement mounting as she panted between kisses, her breath delicious, her scent intoxicating.

He released her only for a moment, retreating two steps towards the ladder they had used to climb up to the loft.

"Where are you going?" she asked.

"I'm not going anywhere," he replied as he descended a couple of steps of the ladder so that his hips were level with the loft's floor. "But you are coming over here!"

She shrieked as he grabbed her ankles and pulled her suddenly towards him so her legs hung over the edge of the loft, nothing but the floor of the barn below them.

"Whatever you do, don't fall!" she cried.

He burst out laughing, and she joined him. They completely lost control, rolling with laughter as he nearly collapsed on top of her. He liked this about her too, the way they could laugh during their lovemaking like friends or secret accomplices as well as lovers.

"I'm not going to fall," he said as he leaned over her, "I'm going to be deep inside you."

"Then I won't let you fall," she uttered in a voice that was almost a moan.

He couldn't remove her clothing fast enough. No patience for his own, he simply freed his manhood, entrusting it to the touch of her adoring hands.

Her legs wrapped around him in a firm and sensual hold.

Neither of them could restrain themselves any longer. He entered her, and they paused for a moment, savoring the first connection of their flesh. He began building up to a furious rhythm, and she urged him on. But he did not let their gratification come too soon...

He slowed, and then began to stroke her sex, wringing tortured moans of extreme pleasure out of her. His hips keeping up their grinding rhythm, he leaned forward to capture her breast in his mouth. He sucked on it, hard, trying to take her even higher. Suddenly, she was quivering around him, gushing, contracting so strongly that she pushed him out of her.

"Oh gods," he panted.

If she only knew how much it drove him wild when she reached her peak. He felt his cock harden even more. When he saw that she had somewhat recovered from the violence of her orgasm, he thrust himself back inside her. Pumping furiously, going as deep inside her as he possibly could, he grasped her breasts in a savage grip. Part of him feared he was hurting her, but he couldn't stop.

She was moaning wildly, he didn't know whether with pain or pleasure. Suddenly he felt the overwhelming climax rip through his body... all thoughts escaped his mind. There was only the terrible delight of the final release, Ariella's devastatingly beautiful body naked before him, and the feeling of pouring himself out into her.

At last, he rested his head on her belly, just breathing.

"Did I hurt you?" he asked, lifting his head to gaze into her beautiful eyes.

She looked up at him, smiling wickedly.

"Yes," she said, "a little. Can we do it again... please?"

CHAPTER 11

Ariella tried fruitlessly to make herself comfortable on a hard and massive wooden chair in the waiting room that adjoined Queen Esclairmonde's throne room. Like most of the castle, the waiting room was cold and drafty, but well lit to ensure that visitors – be they foreign dignitaries, prisoners, nobles, or peasants who had come to resolve a dispute – would be filled with fear and awe at the giant wall carvings that depicted the dynasty's might and power.

On the wall opposite Ariella, Esclairmonde's distant ancestor, King Orrarus, was single-handedly massacring the famous seven barons who had tried to dispute his claim to the throne. It was an ancient tradition that any noble could at any time challenge the reigning monarch to mortal combat and claim the throne, but the kings and queens of Esclairmonde's line had held their own for centuries. On the wall that adjoined the throne room, Ariella beheld the subjugation of the Koroi, who were usually referred to simply as the eastern barbarians. They were depicted in the form of hideous monsters with serpent tails and fanged muzzles. Queen Enelotte, another stern ruler in Esclairmonde's long family line, symbolically subdued them with only a whip in her hand.

The thought suddenly emerged like a kite carried on a strong wind of intuition that kings and queens must be constantly afraid. King Acheron was perhaps an exception, though he had paid with his life for his lack of wariness, not having spotted the serpent within his own household. Looking at the carved stone walls that were supposed to strike fear into the hearts of the vassals, Ariella had the strongest feeling that Queen Esclairmonde was afraid, or at least very insecure.

Ariella had ridden here almost without respite, stopping only to snatch a brief night's rest in her home estate of Leduryon and to gather a few of her trusted warriors. They had then traveled for two days straight and arrived in the capital on the afternoon of the third day. Yet now, Esclairmonde was in no hurry to hear news of the embassy. The Queen's self-important attendant, smiling to show that he knew something she did not, told Ariella that her majesty was occupied with affairs of the state, and so she had been waiting together with the six men and women of her guard for over half an hour.

On the one hand, it might be simply a show of power, giving her extra time to become acquainted with the intimidating carvings. But she sensed it was something more. She recalled Demetrius' warning about the Queen using her like a pawn, or even trying to have her killed. Perhaps behind closed doors, Esclairmonde was debating how to do just that.

Ariella became distracted once again with thoughts of Demetrius. He had haunted her throughout the journey to the capital. His perfect face, his sense of humour, and the sensuality he could exude with one small movement of an eyebrow, one brief gleam of his blue eyes. Despite the anger she had felt on the eve of their parting, thinking of him was a sweet distraction.

That fateful morning, the winds blew fitfully, as if reminding her that it was time to go home. She felt awkward, avoiding Demetrius' gaze as they both climbed down from the hayloft. It had been perhaps their finest night of making love. It had been more raw and savage than anything they had done before, all the sophistication of their previous encounters gone, but they had both shown just how much passion they had for each other. And yet they still knew so little about each other's secrets. Now at last, it was time for them to ride off in different directions.

"Ariella, I will come back for you, I promise," he said.

"Don't make promises you can't keep," she replied.

"Then I promise that you will always be in my thoughts," he offered, "Can you at least believe that?"

She looked up at him, finally able to meet his eyes. "Yes, that is a better promise."

He smiled then in a way she had never seen before. It gave away something of his brave, outrageous, beautiful spirit, a spirit that could survive thirteen years of slavery and still have hope for the future.

She stepped towards him to kiss him, and they embraced with desperate passion that could barely be controlled. Ariella felt the ghost of that kiss still hovering about her lips. She never wanted it to fade.

The queen's attendant interrupted her reminiscence as he solemnly declared: "The queen wishes to see you now, Baroness of Leduryon."

Ariella stood up and followed the officious lackey, nodding briefly to her guards, a sign to stay alert. Etiquette prevented them from following her inside, but they would be ready to burst in if Ariella should give the signal which they had agreed upon, a whistle.

The doors opened sharply to reveal the queen's throne room. The assembled council murmured and stirred as Ariella's name was announced and fell silent as she entered. Once again, Ariella felt a sickening emptiness in the pit of her stomach as she sensed something was off.

Her footsteps echoed off the mosaic tiles of the floor. She felt the stares of the councillors who sat on either side of the walkway. But most of all she felt the piercing gaze of Queen Esclairmonde, who towered over everyone on the dais just in front of her throne. The queen was a little shorter than Ariella, but the height of the platform upon which she stood allowed her to glare down upon her vassal like a stern goddess. She wore a black dress flecked with gold threads and decorated with a jewelled neckline that sparkled with emeralds. On her right hand side sat her sorceress and advisor, Ataros. With smoothly combed white hair and an indulgent smile, Ataros seemed more like some fashionable matron than a dealer of the occult, but everyone knew full well that she was not to be crossed. Her clear blue eyes were like glass. There was no human warmth in them.

Ariella touched down on one knee, her head bowed as was the custom. She could not speak until the queen spoke to her, and now again the queen kept her waiting.

At length, Esclaimonde spoke. "You have taken a long time to get here, only to bring bad news. I do not see your guard. I hear nothing good from Chaldea, and this distresses me greatly. But I would like to know the truth, however harsh it may be. Rise and make your report, baroness."

Ariella had been partly prepared for something to go amiss, but she had not expected the reception to be this unpleasant. As she rose up and met the queen's eyes, she hoped she could still salvage the situation.

"I do not know what news or rumours you have heard, your majesty," she said, "but I rode as swiftly as I could to reach you and make my report. Indeed, the embassy did not go as expected. On the night of my arrival, King Acheron was assassinated."

The councillors burst into exclamations of surprise and shock. These were for the most part elderly barons who had in one way or another found favor with the queen. Ariella wondered how much they knew. Was their reaction completely feigned? Were all their actions completely controlled by the queen?

Esclairmonde unfolded a small scrap of paper that had been clenched in her hand this whole time.

"King Theodos sent me this message," she said dispassionately as if Ariella had not spoken at all, "stating that you rudely demanded that he cede the disputed lands, so that he was forced to refuse in order to maintain his family's honor."

"Your Majesty, if you will allow me to tell you what happened, you shall see that the message is false. I did no such thing."

"Are you accusing a king of being a liar?" Esclairmonde raised her eyebrows.

"King or not, he is trying to deceive you, your majesty," Ariella replied as evenly as she could. "There was no negotiation. I never spoke to–" she nearly choked on the title "King Theodos about the land claim, for I was too busy trying to escape from his assassins."

"Why would King Theodos try to insult me by killing my ambassador? That would be the act of a madman, surely."

"From what I have seen, it is safe to say he is a madman, your majesty," Ariella replied, struggling to keep her voice level, "He had his own father murdered."

Again, the crowd muttered, and Ariella wondered if the assassination was kept so secret that it was known only to those within Theodos's palace.

"I received word that King Acheron was taken ill," Esclairmonde declared, "This killing you talk of is the fruit of an overactive imagination and a fearful disposition. However, it is not your falsehood that troubles me most, but the loss of the guard I had sent to protect your sorry hide. Somehow, you seem to have lost them along the way. They have paid the price for your weakness."

"Your majesty, how can you trust Theodos's word against that of your own envoy?" Ariella exclaimed, "Theodos has betrayed you. It was by his orders that my guards were killed, poisoned."

"Enough of your prevarications," Esclairmonde's voice cut through the hall like a sheet of ice. "I can see exactly how you lost your composure in Chaldea, as you are doing now."

Hearing this, Ariella nearly did lose all composure. A terrible rage seethed within her, but she resisted the impulse to draw her sword and charge at the queen. It would have been so easy to challenge her now, but Ariella doubted she was ready to face such a seasoned warrior.

It was to be expected that Theodos's treachery would reach even here, and she kicked herself for not being more prepared for such a turn of events. What truly amazed her, however, was the queen's demeanor. Though Esclairmonde claimed to be outraged, she looked merely cold and forbidding. Ariella had seen her angry, and this was not it. The council was strangely quiet too. Something was happening under the surface, something which Ariella could not yet comprehend, but she swore to find out the truth very soon.

She looked furtively around the hall for extra guards. There were two behind the throne and two at the door, the usual numbers. Still, Ariella was uneasy, and she stood ready at any moment to whistle for her own guards and make a dash for it just as she had done in Chaldea. Perhaps escaping from royal castles was going to become a habit.

"A harsh punishment is required in a case such as this," the queen continued, "For although you have not committed outright treason, your actions were dishonorable and most injurious to the crown and the kingdom."

Ariella maintained a defiant stance, head held high, but kept silent. She understood that nothing she could say would sway the queen's mind. Someone had already judged and sentenced her, perhaps the queen herself or some other power behind the throne.

The queen signalled to the scribe to begin writing.

"A decree:" she announced. "Baroness of Leduryon, for the high crime of failing in your duty to your sovereign, you are hereby sentenced to exile from the bounds of Dezearre. You may take with you two followers from your personal guard and two domestic servants, but no more than that. You may also take any property you and your servants are able to carry. As for the rest of your property, land, and castle, they are all forfeit to the crown and shall be given to Baroness Jana Ancarette, who has proven herself well on the field of battle."

Ariella felt as if her whole body had turned to stone. All human emotions seemed to have fled her. If she had been guilty of all the crimes Esclairmonde described, perhaps this sentence would have been just, but as things stood, this was one of the harshest penalties a monarch could exact upon a noble who had not committed high treason. The punishment for treason was death, and Ariella wondered in her detached state, why Esclairmonde had not simply sentenced her to death. But then she supposed that such a sentence would require a tribunal and a judgment based on evidence, which Esclairmonde did not likely possess. Ariella sensed that the rest of the council was uncomfortable with the proceedings. They avoided her eyes.

"Is the council in agreement?" Queen Esclairmonde asked.

The elderly councilman who spoke for the collective stood up. "Yes, your majesty. We judge your actions to be for the good of the kingdom."

"Does anyone object?" the queen asked unnecessarily.

The council men and women were silent. No matter how Ariella tried to catch their eyes, they would not meet her gaze. She almost laughed at the travesty of what was happening. The ceding of her land to the baroness of Ancarette was the last drop in the bucket. Ariella had encountered the baroness several times, and each time she had been assured that she knew no one who was a bigger braggart or an altogether more obnoxious person.

There was no choice but to retreat, for now.

Ariella made an exaggeratedly deep bow. "May I retire now to begin preparations for leaving, your majesty?" she asked.

"Yes, you may go," Esclairmonde uttered in a lazy tone, as if she was bored of Ariella's company.

Ariella made another ceremonial bow, turned around, and walked slowly out of the throne room, making sure every step was firm and that her head was still held high.

As she walked, she was mentally assessed her castle's armaments as well as the food and water it could store to sustain a long siege if necessary. For she had decided then and there that she would rather die than see her castle taken away by this most unjust of royal decrees.

The queen had no intention of holding further court, so she swiftly dismissed the council and retreated into the adjoining study together with her sorceress, Ataros.

Esclairmonde paced the study, waving a careless hand for the sorceress to sit down.

"Forget about etiquette, Ataros," she growled, "We have bigger problems to worry about."

"Your majesty, I wish you would have listened to my advice and plainly accused her of treason."

"I know," Esclairmonde declared irritably, "but I still say the risk was too great. Real evidence is needed to accuse a noblewoman, and to have her executed."

She had expected Theodos to take care of that part. He was supposed to have killed her long ago.

"Besides," Esclairmonde continued, spinning around to face the sorceress, "if I exile her, surely she will not interfere with our plans?"

"Your majesty, I have told you that she cannot avoid encountering Theodos again. For it is fated that the two Zaliati be either allies or mortal enemies. We have now set them on course to make them the latter, so one of them is now destined to kill the other. None of this would have happened if your majesty had but considered betting on Ariella instead of that duplicitous prince of Chaldea."

"Are you going to scold me again, Ataros?"

The queen glared at her sorceress, who was unfazed, safe in her knowledge of the occult, that no mortal was a threat to her, not even a queen. Esclairmonde was really more angry with herself. Could she have prevented all of this from spiralling out of control by not sending Ariella on that blasted embassy? Had she been so blinded by mere pride, by vanity?

Perhaps it was true. She recalled seeing Ariella for the first time, a nervous young thing who knew nothing about courtly life. She was prettier than Esclairmonde, more lithe and not exactly graceful, but energetic in a way the queen had been in her prime. Esclairmonde, who was now in her late thirties and beginning to feel the first signs of stiffness in her joints and lines on her face, could not help but feel the sting of envy, especially knowing that this simple young creature was destined to become a legendary warrior. This mere vassal was to inherit the power to defeat entire armies, while Esclairmonde, a queen, was to remain unmarked by such momentous fate. So what if Ariella had the sword of Evrain? In the old days, it was all well and good for a monarch to rule over one hundred people with a few chickens to their name and call themselves a kingdom. The kingdom of Evrain's daughter Yerra was one such community, but over the centuries, her kingdom had lost its splendor and come under Esclairmonde's rule, becoming a subordinate barony. Esclairmonde felt she was born to a greater fate, and ancient traditions would not hold her back.

That was when she had decided to ally herself with Theodos instead. At least he was a crown prince and worthy of the esteem of a fellow monarch. Originally, she had wanted Ariella to negotiate for the land, but she changed her mind in the last moment, sending a letter to Theodos through one of her trusted agents in Chaldea.

Esclairmonde flopped down into a chair, feeling drained.

"How on earth did she escape from that palace? She was alone, her retinue all killed. She was surrounded by Theodos's guards."

"The Zaliati are wondrous warriors," Ataros said wistfully, making Esclairmonde wonder if the sorceress too was guilty of envy. "Even before they begin their training, they have amazing fighting skills and an instinct for survival."

"Do you think she knows the truth about her destiny?" Esclairmonde asked.

Ataros shook her head. "She will not fully come into her powers until the rise of Zalia, ten days from now. It is then that her mentor will step forward to begin training her and will tell her all about her destiny. Theodos' star will rise soon as well."

"At least he has an equal chance then," said the queen. "But if she defeats him?"

"We shall have to fight the winner, in either case," Ataros replied gravely. "And you will be the one to restore the Chaldean Empire, your majesty."

"But how can you be sure?" the queen asked.

Ataros smiled with pure self-indulgence. "My queen, I leave nothing to chance. There is a third star, a wild and wandering star."

She went to the window as if she could see the tiny lights in their firmaments despite it being daytime. "The other two, Zalia and Ti are ancient gods who support the inheritors of old titles, but the third star is stronger than both of them, and it will give its power only to the person who is brave enough to challenge the Zaliati."

Esclairmonde felt inspired. She knew she was destined for greatness, and Ataros had read it in the sky.

"I could also consult the bones if you like, your majesty. Maybe we can find out what really happened in Chaldea."

The queen nodded nervously.

The sorceress untied the pouch that hung at her belt. She dipped her hand inside and drew out the bones she always used for scrying.

Esclairmonde looked away. She did not want to admit to weakness, and she was not exactly frightened, but there was something very unsettling about the ritual. She did not know whose bones they were, and she suspected it was just as well that she didn't. They may have been animal bones, for they were mostly quite small and none of them looked immediately recognizable. But there were a few square shaped ones that Esclairmonde suspected were of human origin, ones that could have once been part of someone's hand or foot.

Ataros threw the bones in the air, and they swirled in a green mist that formed swiftly around them. The queen could not help but be drawn to the sound they made. It was like voices speaking from the farthest ends of the earth or from the deepest trenches of the ocean. She could not understand their language, but they held her in morbid fascination.

Strange shapes formed in the mist, like the vague moldings

made by tea leaves or the traceries of foam conjured by the stormy sea. There was a story in those shapes, but the queen was unable to read it. It made her feel vaguely afraid.

"Well, what is it, Ataros?" she queried impatiently. "How was she able to escape?"

The sorceress continued gazing into the depth of the circle where the bones drifted around, chasing each other.

"She has an ally... someone who has not yet revealed himself as such... a powerful man, a king or a prince..."

"Is it Theodos?" exclaimed Esclairmonde, "Did Theodos spare her?! This was not supposed to be! If they ally, we cannot defeat them."

"Indeed, it would take all my strength to defeat one of them alone," Ataros said bleakly. "But it is too soon to tell. It may not be Theodos who is her ally, but someone else entirely. In fact, I have a feeling it is someone who might appear at first glance to be far removed from these matters."

"Well, who is it?" the queen demanded.

"I cannot say, your majesty. But sooner or later, he will show himself. And if he is not one of the Zaliati, I could easily deal with him."

"Do you see anything that could help us?" the queen urged.

"I believe Theodos did try to kill our baroness. He hates her passionately for standing between him and what he believes to be his legacy, to restore the Chaldean Empire. Though she does not know it yet, they are both bound to vie for the crown, along with the third champion. I will ensure that it is you, my queen."

The queen breathed a sigh of relief. At least thus far, her plan of divide and conquer was working. She needed for the two Zaliati to fight each other. She needed Theodos to be on her side, for the time being.

"Do you think she will obey my decree of exile?" the queen suddenly asked. "I thought I detected a smirk of defiance in that smug face."

"She will leave Dezearre, even if she does not intend to," Ataros stated. "The bones have said so."

"And when she is beyond our borders," Esclairmonde mused, "perhaps she could meet with an untimely death that would be in no way connected to the crown of Dezearre…"

CHAPTER 12

The first onslaught of the autumn wind whipped up the flags on the castle walls, and it seemed bitterly appropriate that on this day the watchmen sighted Baroness Ancarette approaching, a column of fifty riders in gleaming armor streaming behind her.

Ariella was alerted at once; everyone from the smallest child to the captain of the guards knew of the looming danger, and they all stood firmly with her, determined to fight rather than surrender to a new wilful and capricious mistress.

As soon as the guards reported to Ariella, she hurried towards the battlements, a couple of slender swifthounds trailing her, whining softly as they sensed the sudden change in her mood.

Ariella had neglected to wear a warm cloak, but she hardly felt the piercing chill of the wind as she stood upon the walls in her shirt and leather tunic. Anger stirred her blood until she felt her face flush with a burning sensation she had thought only lust was capable of producing. The rider at the head of the column advanced towards her castle with unruffled confidence. Even from this distance Ariella recognized the excessive self-assurance of her posture, as well as those unmistakably insolent green eyes and lush red curls. Ancarette was about ten years older than Ariella and much more experienced in battle, but to look at her strutting and swaggering, she may as well have been seventeen.

The rider was not even looking in her direction. It was fair to assume that Ancarette was still blissfully ignorant of the fact that this castle, bestowed upon her so generously by the queen, was still occupied by its former baroness.

At last, she came right up to the castle gate, obviously expecting it to be opened for her.

"Up there in the castle!" Ancarette's strong, deep voice carried well to the topmost towers. "Is this how you greet your new baroness?"

Ariella took a deep breath. This was the first active step she would take in her rebellion.

"The castle isn't yours, not yet," she replied.

Ancarette craned her head to see where the voice was coming from.

"Baroness of Leduryon?" she shouted in disbelief.

"Yes, Baroness of Ancarette?" Ariella replied with mock civility.

"I thought you would be shuffling off into exile by now."

Ariella smiled. "Life is full of disappointment, isn't it?"

Ancarette quickly regained her sense of confidence. "I had heard that you dishonoured our land and done a disservice to the queen, but I did not think you had the gall for all-out rebellion."

"If by 'rebellion' you mean I'm no longer a follower of that vile serpent you call a queen, then you are correct. My blood is noble, and I can live by my own rule if I so choose. I am no one's servant."

"Bold words!" Ancarette remarked. "But really, enough of your posturing, Ariella. You know as well as I do that you're not a powerful baroness with sprawling territories and armies at your command. You do realize that I will take what's mine?"

"You may try," Ariella shrugged.

"And who will defend your castle, the scullery maid?"

"Maybe. But that's not your concern."

"Isn't it, though? I will be the one to take this castle, and I don't want my future servants injured and my property damaged. I have the feeling a lot of blood will be spilled here if you persist in this madness. And the saddest part of it is, if you fight me, I will not be able to spare your life. I spare no one who rebels against the queen."

"Nobody asked you to," Ariella replied. "If you are so sure of defeating me, why are we still talking?"

"Because I fear you don't understand that by refusing my claim to the castle you have sealed your fate."

"Have I?"

"If you surrender now, I am willing – despite your rebellion – to grant you the same terms Queen Esclairmonde has."

"That is very generous," Ariella let sarcasm drip from every word, "but even if I did decide to leave the home of my ancestors and surrender it to you, I would prefer to take all my people with me."

"I'm trying to be patient," Ancarette declared with an edge in her voice, "but I cannot grant what the queen herself has denied."

"Then I cannot agree to your terms," Ariella said, anger flashing in her voice, "I thought I was talking to a noblewoman, but I see you are just the queen's lapdog. Do you always do whatever she commands?"

"Good, keep piling on the insults," Ancarette replied with a menacing smirk, "I will remember them when you are begging for your life."

Ariella knew the negotiation was over. In her mind, it was a waste of time. Ancarette did her best to avoid a siege, of course, because keeping the castle surrounded and scaling the walls would cost her in resources and fighters probably much more than it would for Ariella, but ultimately Ariella knew that Ancarette's pride would not let her rest until she had at least tried to claim her prize. A real siege was inevitable.

She also counted on the queen to stay out of the dispute. Although it was by the queen's command that the castle was supposed to be ceded, it would dishonor Ancarette if she could not claim her own domain without outside help.

"I intend to send for reinforcements now, and they will arrive within two days. If you dare not face us in open combat, you will be a prisoner in your own castle. I can besiege you here for as long as I like," Ancarette boasted.

Ariella did not completely believe that. Of course, reinforcements would arrive. Ancarette commanded almost twice the number of warriors that Ariella did. However, they could not be obligated to serve indefinitely, since most barons could enlist their fighters to serve in active warfare for only a few months of any given year. Then, there was the coming winter, not a pleasant time to be besieging a castle. The frosts and disease would pose more of a danger to Ancarette's people than they would to Ariella's. They would be snug and warm in the castle, while Ancarette would be shivering in a tent. Ariella felt confident that if she could hold out until the first snowfall, her enemies would have to retreat and give up the siege.

"This castle is strong enough to withstand a thousand sieges. Now, I'm finished negotiating. If sometime in the future you think you can have my attention again, I would be happy to revisit the subject."

Ariella could not repress a tiny smile as she turned away, and walked off, leaving Ancarette to fume below. Being brusquely dismissed was not something to which this baroness was accustomed.

Ariella walked back to her chambers. Her assurance quickly faded as she wondered what would become of her domain in the future. Even if she withstood the siege, would Queen Esclairmonde herself eventually try to enforce the sentence of exile?

Perhaps in that case, Ariella thought, it would be best to take all her people and leave this land, however much it would hurt her to abandon her family's castle, with all the memories it held of her parents and grandparents. And then what would they all become? A roving troop of vagabonds?

There was another option, the unthinkable one, yet Ariella caught herself dwelling on it: to challenge Esclairmonde for the kingdom. Images of the horrible carvings came unbidden to her mind. She would become another casualty of the dynasty, another failed challenger, another cautionary tale.

But maybe not… Maybe, if she had time to train, if she had truly inherited Evrain's sword, surely the queen would be no match for her.

Ariella reached her study, and once inside, she leaned back against the cool stone wall, trying to gather her thoughts.

"My lady, are we disturbing you?"

It was Jaquelle, sporting one of her usual shapeless black dresses, followed closely by the captain of the guards. Jaquelle, despite her years, was more beautiful and more poised than most young women of Leduryon, and no frumpy dress could hide it. She gracefully stepped over a sleeping swifthound as she entered the chamber.

Helnom, the captain of the guard, had served Ariella's parents in that role, and had distinguished himself when the Koroi tribes had attacked the castle, before Ariella was even born. He always inspired her confidence despite his grizzled locks and incredibly wrinkled visage.

"No, come in," Ariella said, greeting them with a weary smile.

"My lady, we wanted to speak with you about the coming assault," Helnom began in his level voice.

"You haven't decided to surrender already, have you Helnom?" Ariella asked jovially, slapping his bony shoulder.

"My lady, that is one option," the captain replied respectfully. "In fact, I was about to advise you to negotiate for peace. It's not too late."

"Helnom!" Ariella chided, "That's not funny!"

Then she realized, judging by the unperturbed look on his face, that he was in earnest.

"Why?" she exclaimed, "Jaquelle, are you with him on this? When did you decide this?"

"We have just seen that Baroness Ancarette is willing to spare no expense on this siege," Jaquelle stepped in, "and you did not help matters by provoking her."

"Oh really, Jaquelle, I don't think it would have made any

difference. She will stop at nothing to take what is supposedly hers."

"Lives may be lost, Ariella," Jaquelle said.

"And what will these lives be like if all these people fall under Ancarette's rule?"

Ariella knew she appeared the foolish young firebrand in the face of their prudent advice. Perhaps they were right, but she simply did not have the heart to abandon the castle and its people to the whims of another ruler.

"Very well then," Jaquelle said in her soothing, maternal voice. "It shall be as you wish. We're with you."

"However, Jaquelle and I have talked it over," Helnom said, "and we thought it would be wise to contact your allies."

"My allies?" Ariella said with a mirthless laugh. "As if the neighbouring barons would come to my aid! They're staying comfortably neutral. If I had time to raise a real rebellion against the queen, maybe they would join my cause, but I'm not ready."

"We are not speaking of them," Jaquelle replied calmly, "but of the allies you have made on your journey. The elf king was a friend to you."

"Bringing the elves here would surely turn the neighbouring barons against us," Ariella responded.

"It may," Jaquelle assented, "though they may have to weigh their cowardice against their dislike of the elves."

"It cannot be," Ariella stated firmly, "the elves are not to be fully trusted. They can read our minds as easily as a book, but I can't read theirs. And who knows what price they would demand for their help?"

"Then there is Prince Demetrius of Sylcadia," Helnom suggested.

Ariella froze at the mention of that name. As if she had not thought of him hundreds of times in a day, as if she had not whispered his name late at night when dreaming of his embrace... Of course she had considered asking for his help; in fact, he had already offered it before they parted. She knew Demetrius' concern for her was real. But to have him leave his kingdom for her sake would without a doubt rekindle their affair, and she could not have that.

Ariella realized that her silence was perhaps too telling.

"No," she said. "We cannot involve him. Why did you tell everyone about him?" she accused Jaquelle.

She had told Jaquelle most of the story, except the parts about her nights with Demetrius and the pleasure theater, but she felt as if the older woman could see right through her. Still, she had been through a lot and the last thing she needed were motherly lectures about men.

Jaquelle would often take on that role as she had done since Ariella's mother died. Now that Ariella was a young woman, Jaquelle no longer had as much sway over her, but she still grumbled and upbraided her lady for "gallivanting around." Although as the baroness, Ariella was free to disregard the words of her former nursemaid, was even free to dismiss her from service and exile her from the domain if she so wished, both of them knew that she could never do that. Still, there had been much tension between them in recent years, and they were not as close as they once had been.

Just before Ariella had left for Chaldea, Jaquelle had been quite unimpressed after walking in on her in bed with a mere nineteen-year-old, and Ariella had thrown a bottle at her. Of course, Jaquelle was too fast and the bottle never hit her, but nevertheless it had been a poor parting, and their reunion on Ariella's return had not been a warm one.

"I didn't tell everyone," Jaquelle said, "only our captain of the guard, because it's important."

"I don't see how it's even relevant," Ariella declared. "He's not here, and he cannot have anything to do with this."

"From what you have told me, it sounds like he owes you a debt," Jaquelle argued hotly, "and if you let him know that you're in dire straits, he will come to your aid."

Yes, Ariella thought, and that is what I'm afraid of.

"We're not in dire straits yet, are we?"

CHAPTER 13

It was a full moon, and although night had long since fallen, everything was illuminated clearly. Ariella looked down from her castle walls as she had done countless times in the last few days. She wore a fur-lined cloak as cold northern winds were blowing. Yet the weather did not deter Ancarette and her troops. Already they had set up their own pickets and guards to prevent the castle's inhabitants from surprising them with a sudden foray. Fresh warriors arrived daily, pitching their tents and lighting fires on her land. These were not just the baroness's household guards but also mercenaries she had hired, for Ancarette did not have this many warriors of her own.

Two weeks had passed since Jaquelle and the captain of the guards had suggested the idea of sending a message to Demetrius, and Ariella was no closer to a resolution on that matter.

She felt like she had declared war upon the whole world, all except one man, whom she could never have.

She thought her ardor for the prince would have cooled long ago, but even now as she gazed down on the cold wintry plain, she could see his face, hear his voice as if he were here with her. The strength of his armies would surely be a boon in the face of Ancarette's siege, but she found herself dwelling on the sound of his laughter, which would have been an incredible comfort to her now, the smoothness of his lips, and the gentleness of his hands.

Aside from Demetrius, while preparing for the siege she had also often thought of her parents, how much love they had for each other, how much stronger it made them in their final days. But would her feelings for Demetrius be her strength or her ultimate weakness?

There was no ease in the siege, as Jaquelle had warned. There were nightly patrols, and the cries of the sentries that all was quiet, and worries about supplies lasting through the winter. But so far, Ancarette had not made any move.

The unsettling sound of hammering reached Ariella from below. Ancarette's people were constructing siege engines, and the work rarely stopped. Even now, they were hammering by torchlight. As she turned to go back inside, a new sound cut through the chill night air. Cries from the warriors camped below. At first, she could not make them out. Then she saw a shadow flit through the air, a ragged shape gliding on the wind, making for the castle.

Then she knew what the cries were: "Glider! Glider!"

Two arrows whistled through the darkness.

Then more cries: "Kill it! Don't let it reach the castle!"

Ariella's heart froze. The arrows missed their mark, and the glider continued cutting through the air, all too well illuminated by the round moon. It was a creature no bigger than a squirrel, but extremely valuable for its skill in traveling long distances and finding a recipient. This had to be an important message, Ariella thought. In any case, the besiegers believed it was, for more arrows swarmed in the night.

They had little hope of hitting such a small, moving creature, but the sheer magnitude of their volley looked like it might overwhelm the little flyer. Arrows bounced off the castle wall, but Ariella did not duck or step away from the parapet. Her eyes followed the shadowy form. She didn't know whether it was intuition or simply wishful thinking, but she had a feeling that the message was from Demetrius.

It cost a fortune to train one of those creatures, and it involved a wizard to point them in the direction of a certain person or location. Only a prince or a very rich baron could afford such an expense. Besides, who else would be willing to go through the trouble for her?

She gripped the ice-cold stones of the battlement. The glider was now almost within reach, only about thirty feet away. Suddenly, it spun out of control and fell. It must have been hit by one of the myriad of arrows. A cheer went up from the besiegers, and Ariella pounded her fist on the wall.

But then a new sound was heard as the cheers died down. The sound of wings fighting air currents. Ariella was afraid to hope again, but as she looked down, she saw the poor little creature beating its wings to fight its way up. She could tell it was wounded, its flight spasmodic and uneven, but at last it secured another air current and glided upwards in an arc.

She could see the moonlight reflected in its eye as it came toward her. The warriors below must have been too stunned by this recovery, they released no more arrows. Ariella gasped as the creature flew straight towards her. Instinctively, she caught it as it landed right in her hands. She felt its soft fur and a trickle of warm blood. Its heartbeat pounded much faster than hers, even though hers was racing. Its eyes still reflected the terror of its flight, and its nose sniffed her hands, satisfied that she was the right recipient.

At once, she ran down to the main hall, cradling the messenger in her hands. She set it down on an old wooden bench close to the fireplace and called for the servants to find Jaquelle at once. Jaquelle had the healing power. She would know what to do.

The creature's chest and one of its wings had been grazed by an arrow. She could not tell how deep the cut was, only that it may have hit vital organs in its body and crippled part of the wing. Luckily, it had not been a direct hit, and the arrow was not lodged in the wound.

A piece of parchment had been tied carefully around the glider's hind leg, and Ariella removed it gingerly, without jostling the wounded animal.

"What's the matter?"

Ariella heard Jaquelle's voice and could breathe again.

"Here's a patient for you," Ariella said, attempting a smile.

Jaquelle smiled back in that reassuring way she had. She kneeled by the bench, gently inspecting the injured wing. The glider made no protest and seemed to relax into her weathered hands.

"Well, will he live?" Ariella inquired impatiently.

"With the gods' help," Jaquelle replied. "And he may yet fly again."

Ariella breathed a sigh of relief. She had always had faith in Jaquelle's ability. Ever since Ariella could remember, when she had skinned her knee or accidentally got a deep cut in training, Jaquelle would soothe her with calming words and miraculously cure the wound with her magical balms.

Now, as Jaquelle carried the creature to her chamber, Ariella had no doubt she would see it again whole and healthy. She was eager for its recovery not only for the sake of the brave little animal but also because she had no gliders of her own, and she needed to send a message back to Demetrius. She had not read his words yet, but the mere fact that he sent this message meant that he had not forgotten her. He had not forgotten his promise of keeping her in his thoughts.

Ariella clutched the slip of parchment that she had taken off the glider's leg. She went up to her chamber, a candle in hand. When she set the candle down in a holder and sat down on the bed, drawing a deep breath, she finally unfurled the letter and read it.

My dearest,

I will abide by your request. I will not dare to hope for your affection until I have settled my affairs here. Alas, I am still engaged. As I had supposed, it will take time. Still, be not angry with me for offering once again to come and see you in Dezearre. My only thought is your happiness and safety. Give but the word, and I will fly to your side.

I love you,

D

He had not written her name probably in case the message was intercepted, but it was obviously for her and no one else.

The last words of the letter made her body tingle all over. He had never plainly said he loved her. Now that she saw those words written on a parchment for which the little glider had risked its life, Ariella wanted to believe they were true. But the hot surge of emotions was doused when she remembered the rest of the message. Nothing had really changed. Demetrius was still prince of Sylcadia, and he was still engaged. How many times she wished he was still just a runaway slave, her mysterious companion on their perilous journey!

She needed his help, but she did not have the strength to make that decision yet. There had been enough excitement for one night, she decided.

She folded up the parchment, stored it inside a small chest on her nightstand, and tried to forget about it for the moment. What she really needed was sleep. All answers would come to her in the morning.

Yet sleep eluded her. In fact, it was nowhere to be found. She lay back on the bed still dressed, and her mind was racing. She was ridiculously tired, but the excitement of the night had somehow given her fresh energy, of a nervous and restless kind. It would be better to get up and keep watch on the walls instead. Just then, someone knocked at her door.

"Enter," she called.

It was Jaquelle. She was composed on the surface but Ariella could tell she was buzzing with excitement. On the days when Jaquelle trained in swordplay, she wore a sword at her side and a dark tunic over her strong, sturdy frame, just as drab as her usual dresses, but it did nothing to conceal the beauty of her face and her long black hair.

"Come with me," Jaquelle stated without preamble.

"Anywhere in particular?"

"Someplace where we can see the night sky," Jaquelle

allowed, "It is your twenty-fifth birthday."

"I can hardly think about that now," Ariella grumbled.

"But you must."

Her tone was incontrovertible, and although Ariella had long since ceased to follow Jaquelle's instructions, she obeyed now.

They went up to the roof of the highest tower. From here, the besieging army was like so many ants. Their fires blazed below like glow worms.

Jaquelle pointed the eastern horizon, where a tiny red speck was hovering in the black sky.

"That's Zalia, the crimson star. Zalia chose your soul before you were even born. She appeared once before on the day of your birth, and she will rise now, starting with your twenty-fifth birthday. When she reaches her zenith, your destiny will be revealed."

And then Ariella felt a strange shift take place. This was no longer that nervous, miserable energy that wouldn't let her sleep. The newly awakened strength that now pounded through her veins like molten fire and roused her for battle. It came not only from the star itself, but from all around, from the forest, from the plains, from the distant centuries when heroes strove with immortal elves.

"It is time," Jaquelle said.

She drew her short sword and lunged at Ariella.

Only it seemed that Jaquelle was moving towards her with incredible slowness. Not having her sword with her, Ariella could only dodge and deflect. To evade the attack, she pivoted and stepped to the side, which was all she could do in the small platform atop the tower. Jaquelle's blade clanged against stone.

"Good!" Jaquelle said. "I'll try again."

Again she lunged. Ariella knew that Jaquelle could be devilishly fast. It was Jaquelle who had first trained her when she was only a child. Other teachers soon followed, but Jaquelle was now the only one who posed any challenge.

And yet, now she was easily able to best her original teacher. She stepped to the side, blocking the blade with the leather armor on her right forearm. Then she daringly seized Jaquelle's wrist and twisted the blade out of her grasp.

"Jaquelle, are you trying to raise my morale by letting me win?"

The older woman shook her head. She was grinning mysteriously.

"What?"

"You've just gotten a taste of power, but you'll have to work hard to achieve its full potential. This rush of strength is now yours because the star that favors you has just appeared over the horizon. The next time you will feel this strong, the star will be at its highest place in the sky. You will not be as strong or as fast in the next few days, but I think you are now ready to learn more."

"More? I hardly know anything. Why have you kept me in the dark, Jaquelle, about the Zaliati, about everything?"

Instead of replying, Jaquelle attacked again, striking with her fists. Ariella could barely keep up with the barrage, but she managed to block each punch. Following an instinct to fight back, she struck out, and managed to hit Jaquelle's cheekbone, knocking her against the cold stone wall. It was only then she realized how angry she was.

Jaquelle's look of astonishment made her feel instantly guilty. They would not normally go for the face when they practiced. They stood there for a while, glaring at each other, panting.

Jaquelle broke the silence.

"Maybe I should have told you everything, but I didn't know your diplomatic mission would lead you into a trap. At least the things I did teach you helped you fight your way free."

"I'm sorry," Ariella said.

"It's all right." Jaquelle grinned, feeling her cheekbone carefully. "Pain only awakens our fighting spirit."

"But why didn't you tell me?" Ariella demanded.

"Too much knowledge would have been dangerous for you," Jaquelle said, "It would have done more harm than good to have you brooding on these things. I know you. Your mind can become obsessive."

"And so you let me brood instead on my parents' death when I could have been thinking about my future?"

Jaquelle crossed her arms. She didn't raise her voice. She hardly ever did. If anything, she now spoke softer but with more assurance than ever.

"My dear, you've long ago stopped brooding on your parents and started thinking more about how much wine you can vomit and how many men you can sleep with. Do you think it didn't torment me keeping it a secret, especially when I saw you day after day wasting your time and killing your spirit?"

"Well, why didn't you?" Ariella cried.

"You've spoken with Queen Esclairmonde. She knows about your destiny, it's obvious now, or else she would not have tried to have you killed."

"So?"

"She must think of nothing but taking that power for herself. Do you think she sleeps easy at night? I didn't want that for you. I didn't want you to know that you had a mortal enemy from the very time you were born. You were not ready. I don't even think you're ready now."

Ariella wanted to insist that she was, but she sensed that Jaquelle was probably right.

"I never wanted an empire…" she muttered.

"Good," Jaquelle said.

"So it is true, the ancient writing in the tale of Evrain, 'if the empire should wane' as it is now, 'seek the Alchemist to help restore peace, restore the empire'?"

"Yes. But one thing you must know…" Jaquelle pronounced, "There is another star, another god, who will favour another warrior. This star is called Ti and it will rise in a few days. Someone else will turn twenty five on that night."

Suddenly, Ariella knew. She felt it in her blood though she wished with all her heart she didn't. She knew before Jaquelle said it.

"King Theodos."

CHAPTER 14

Five days after the first sighting of Zalia, Ancarette attempted to bombard the walls, only to fail miserably. At first, the shaking of the outer wall and the noise of the stones crashing against it frightened Leduryon's inhabitants, but almost at once they realized that Ancarette's catapults were too weak to launch the stones much farther than the outer wall of the castle. A few missiles landed in the courtyard, but they could not hit the main keep at all. Even when they did manage to hit one of the castle walls, the stones crumbled against its ancient bricks.

Ariella stood proudly on the battlements, disdaining the missiles. She looked towards the horizon at the crimson star, willing it to rise higher. Her guards laughed at the enemy's pathetic siege engines. She liked that. It might taunt Ancarette into attempting an escalade and actually risking a real battle. Ariella felt ready for it. Her strength and speed had returned to more or less normal levels, nowhere near what they had been the night Zalia first rose in the sky. Even so, Ariella had more strength than ever before, and she knew she would only get stronger. Her spirits were lifted now that she knew her power was real, not just something that was talked and plotted about behind her back.

"Well, we may as well go down for dinner," she finally said

as another ineffectual missile bounced off the outer wall.

It was rewarded with a burst of laughter from the guards. They all walked down to the dining hall, leaving only the watchmen on the walls.

As she neared the dining hall, she heard the familiar strains of 'Hand me my trusty bow', an ancient and melancholy tune. It was a song Helnom favored most nights, and his deep voice gave it a moving interpretation.

Hand me my trusty bow,
If I should fall, my bow in hand
The archer's soul will fly like an arrow
To the Blessed Lands.

Still, Ariella wished he would sometimes allow a little variety in his choice of songs. She thought wistfully of the bawdy verses Mara had sung in the forest.

She had expected it to be a most routine dinner, but as she entered the hall, Ariella's heart fluttered in her chest. The glider was flitting about beneath the ceiling to the amusement of the populace. Its wounds had healed incredibly well thanks to Jaquelle's ministrations. Perhaps it would soon be ready to make a long distance flight.

Ariella sat down in her usual seat, and suddenly she felt the touch of little paws as the glider alighted on her shoulder. It chittered in her ear and sniffed her hair.

"Soon you'll be free to fly," she said, stroking its back.

She tried to compose a message to Demetrius in her mind. All she could think was please come! I need you.

Just as she was climbing the stairway to her bedchamber, the silvery sound of horns alerted her to a new danger. Emelote, a sturdy guardswoman in her thirties, breathless from running, reported to her.

"My lady, Ancarette is leading an escalade. She has shot three arrows at our castle gate to signal the attack."

So she had not misjudged her foe after all. Ancarette's pride must have been wounded by the siege engines' failure. And Ariella could not wait to face such an unbalanced and weakened adversary.

"She has my attention now," she muttered.

Helnom had been summoned too, and he joined Ariella on the windswept walls.

"Shall we get to work?" Ariella asked him.

"All is ready, my lady," he replied. "We have prepared for this."

The night was cloudy, and it was barely possible to see the enemy approach. They were like vague shades darker than the night, milling beneath the walls. Helnom placed his archers all around the outer perimeter. There were no weak points in the well-built stonework, nothing that could be undermined or broken down, and so the enemy would most likely try to climb over the walls. They could strike from any and all directions.

The archers were at a disadvantage because of the poor light, but they would have to try their luck. Helnom commanded them to begin shooting at the advancing enemy. The twanging of bows filled the chilly night air. Arrows zoomed downward, and bloodcurdling screams from below testified to successful hits.

The next sound to fill the cold night air was the thudding of ladders upon the battlements. The guards hurried over to try to push these away. Sometimes they succeeded, but some of the ladders had been so firmly entrenched that nothing could move them.

That was fine, Ariella thought. Let them come.

More screams from below as deadly arrows twanged. Bodies thudding to the ground. The battle cries of Ancarette's warriors almost drowned out the wailing of the wounded.

Before Ariella realized what was happening, she found herself putting on her heavy helmet and rushing towards the first attackers who were appearing upon the walls. Her guards were already hacking at them, trying to push them down, where many fell to their deaths.

She ran to the eastern wall, where the attackers came in greater numbers. They had not yet overwhelmed the guards that were posted there, but they began to outnumber Ariella's people. She charged at the nearest invader, reversing the grip on her sword and hammering him with the pommel. The man tottered, but righted himself just in time, preventing a fall off the battlements, only to be stabbed at once by one of Ariella's guards.

Seeing that this opponent was down, Ariella spun around just in time to ward off two enemy swords. Two warriors advanced on her, trying to pin her against the wall. She sank into a low crouch, then slashed at one of them, forcing him to move aside. Her blade cut through the other opponent's leg armor, and he fell forward into the castle's courtyard.

The familiar excitement of battle was on her. It was not an angry sensation, but rather like something a gambler might feel when on a winning streak.

The smell of boiling pitch filled the air. Her fighters poured the burning liquid down from the walls upon the attackers, and even louder screams sounded from below.

Without any conscious thought, she cut down three opponents in as many seconds. Her instincts were ruling her body.

"Ancarette! Where are you?" Ariella shouted. She had not meant to even say it out loud, but the intoxication of battle was sweeping her straight into its spinning maelstrom.

Then she looked down onto the gatehouse, and the realization of what was happening poured over her like a bucket of ice water. Ancarette was no coward, but she had no intention of losing her life to a stray arrow in the storming. She was probably waiting for her troops to penetrate the wall and open the drawbridge so that she could ride in with her main forces. The invaders were gathering there, trying to make their way to the winches that controlled the portcullis and the drawbridge.

The area around the gatehouse was quickly turning into a melee. Ancarette's warriors desperately sought to lower the bridge. One of them already had his hand on the lever when he was stabbed in the back and fell beside three of his comrades.

Ariella fearlessly waded into the mass, scattering the enemy with scissoring strokes.

Her own warriors were making a stand with their backs against the gatehouse, and Ariella carved a bloody path towards them, dividing the enemy ranks with heavy sweeps of her sword. They tried to close their ranks around her and push her down with their shields, but she nearly laughed at these attempts. She evaded their attack, finding the cracks in their armor and stabbing their vulnerable flesh with the point of her sword.

She finally reached her warriors, clustering together in a tight circle.

"Attack!" Ariella shouted to her people, "Drive them out of our fortress!"

She still had one weapon that was reserved for such desperate straits, the red crystal. It flew from her hand, the force of the red shards pushing the enemy back like a tidal wave. Some fell and some stumbled back upon their comrades. Armor clanged against armor in awful cacophony, and panic engulfed the enemy.

This was just what her people had needed to take heart.

Ariella nearly lost her footing as she sprang forward with the added momentum of her own warriors advancing behind her. Quickly, she caught the crystal again, and the shards coalesced in her hand, just in time. The enemy warriors who had been knocked down charged again, clashing with her troops with furious speed.

It was a close-quarter fight. The smell of blood and sweat suffocated her. She could feel her own sweat soaking right through her shirt and tunic.

A female warrior came out of nowhere with a piercing screech, driving the pommel of her sword into Ariella's face. All she could do was try to duck. The impact was shocking. The woman had just missed the lower exposed part of Ariella's face, but her helmet still took a harsh blow. She stumbled to the side, completely off balance. Right into the chaos of enemy swords...

A strong pair of hands pulled her upright, one of her

warriors, Emelote, the same woman who had first reported the attack. Ariella regained her balance quickly, but she saw that by helping her, Emelote left herself open to an attack, a sword about to slice at her neck. Ariella lunged forward, parrying the deadly blow. Emelote made a thrust at the attacker, aiming low at his thigh. Her sword pierced the leather armour and drew blood.

The man collapsed, falling back onto his fellow warriors.

Ariella's head was still ringing from the blow, but she had no time to recover. Merciless swords flew at her. She fought on without thought, deflecting each deadly weapon, finding a weak point, striking, and slashing.

When she dared to look up, she could see more enemies climbing over the walls, and a fierce struggle for the scant space on the battlements. But the important thing was to hold the gatehouse, not to let them open the gate... Her whole body ached with exhaustion.

She was so tired that she simply tackled her next opponent, landing on top of her. Without the strength to swing a sword, Ariella drew one of her knives and held it to the enemy's vulnerable neck.

"Surrender," she demanded.

"I surrender," said a thin voice from the helmet, the voice of a young girl.

Ariella wondered who would have sent this young one into battle, or whether she had volunteered herself, the latter being most likely. She availed herself of the young woman's sword.

The tide of the fight had swept away from the gate and deeper into the courtyard, but Ariella could see now her warriors stomping out the last vestiges of resistance from the now outflanked assailants.

"What is your name?" she asked the young woman.

"It's not important," came the mumbled reply.

Ariella pulled off her captive's helmet, revealing a rich cascade of hair that shone red in the moonlight.

"Are you part of Ancarette's family?" she asked.

The girl nodded. "I am her niece."

At last, there was a strange stillness all around.

No more attackers coming at her. None in the courtyard, none on the walls, except dead bodies. Beside her, one of Ancarette's men stared blankly at the sword stuck in his belly, too shocked even to scream. A guard dealt him a fatal stab of mercy, piercing his heart. A few wounded warriors uttered moans of pain, and these seemed to be the only sounds in the suddenly still fortress.

Ariella stood up. She raised her sword high in the air and saluted her warriors.

She called out so all of them could hear, "Warriors of Leduryon, you have stood your ground bravely this night."

They did not cheer; she had not expected them to. It was obvious they had suffered too many losses, and many of the warriors left standing were wounded and looked ready to collapse, but they raised their weapons in a silent salute to their leader and to their fallen friends.

Ariella walked up the stairs to the battlement to post a few guards there for the night, though it was unlikely Ancarette would attack again anytime soon.

She had expected to see Helnom, and it took her a few moments to realize that he was not one of the guards left standing.

Helnom had fallen. Of all things, she had never thought this would be possible. Ariella felt the blood pounding in her ears, even stronger now than it had during the battle. Time suddenly slowed to a torturous pace as she ran to his side past the beleaguered guards and the torches and the bloodstains on the castle wall.

"Please, do not move me," she heard him say, "My time has come. Let me die upon the walls here, where I fought."

At last, Ariella reached him and took his shrivelled hand. It was still warm, and his grip was firm.

"I hope I haven't failed you, my lady," he murmured, looking up at her with his ever-present calmness.

Ariella shook her head vigorously. "Of course not, Helnom. How could you possible think you've failed? We repelled their attack. We could hold out here for as long as we like."

"I knew we would," he whispered hoarsely. "It was a grand battle, and your parents would have been proud. Now, I leave you knowing that you will survive this and go on to far greater things."

"No, Helnom. What will I do without my captain?" Ariella tried to coax him.

"I must leave," he replied, his voice growing ever fainter, "This is a good way for me to go, after a glorious battle. Now, I go to the Blessed Lands. Farewell…"

The tired and shocked guards who had gathered round him all looked down in disbelief. Many had tears in their eyes. Ariella did not, for she was too angry, and she could not quite be convinced that he was gone, that no one would be there to sing "Hand me my trusty bow" in the dining hall. Somehow, she had believed Helnom would always be there.

"Take him inside," she said softly.

The moonless night slowly turned into a dull, grey morning. Like many of her people, Ariella was able to snatch a couple hours' sleep, but it was an uneasy rest. She had appointed Emelote, the woman who had come to her aid in the melee, to replace Helnom as captain of the guards. It was not merely because of her help in that single battle; Emelote was always there, ready to help. She had done countless similar deeds. Now as Ariella counted her losses, she was heartbroken: twelve of her warriors dead, and ten wounded.

The dining hall was silent and dark, and few people were eating.

"Perhaps it would have been better to surrender the castle rather than witness its slow demise," Ariella said to Jaquelle as they sat at dinner.

Her mentor looked sleep-deprived and weary from tending the wounded, dark hair tangled and tied back in haphazard fashion.

"It's never too late to surrender," Jaquelle shrugged, "but I am amazed you would say that after we so successfully repelled the invaders. Their losses were far greater than ours, and I doubt they will try another escalade any time soon."

"How can you say that when we've lost Helnom?" Ariella asked.

"I feel his loss too," Jaquelle admitted, "but there are always losses. You are too young to have experienced many of them, but they are inevitable. I know, it was one thing to think about them, to expect them even, and quite a different thing to experience them, especially with Helnom gone."

A few more of the guards trickled into the hall. Their conversation was low and sluggish, lacking the usual banter.

As breakfast came to a close, the men and women of the guards started up a song, and the rest of the people soon joined in. They did not have any accompaniment, but their voices were perfect for this lonesome, melancholy tune. They were singing "Hand me my trusty bow."

A young guard whose clothes were besprinkled with snow came over to Ariella.

"My lady, Ancarette herself is approaching the walls," he reported, "She carries a white flag and wishes to speak with you."

"Well, this is new," Ariella remarked.

It was a sight that was hard to believe. The Baroness of Ancarette riding all alone upon a grey steed with a white flag. It looked somewhat eerie. Ariella rode across the drawbridge and down the hill towards her, knowing that Destiny would bear her swiftly away if this were some trick.

The first scant snowflakes of the season were falling lightly onto the withered grass.

"You wish to talk, Jana?" Ariella began.

"I have a proposition to make," Ancarette replied. "Now, I admit that you have held out well. You gave us a fine display of martial bravery the previous night."

"A display," Ariella chuckled, "I'd say we gave you a sound thrashing."

"Well, whatever you choose to think about it," Ancarette continued, raising her chin proudly, "I have decided that I have wasted enough time here. And after all, it is only a matter of time before you succumb to our superior numbers. So, I'm looking for a way to end this siege."

"I'm listening," Ariella said.

"Ariella, Baroness of Leduryon, I challenge you to single combat. If the gods favor you, you will keep your castle and your land. If I win, the land, the castle, and everything in it will be mine."

Ariella had not expected this. She suddenly realized that Ancarette was even more desperate than she had originally thought. She must be running out of funds or maybe her warriors wanted to go home for the winter. She had not mentioned her niece at all. Too proud to beg, even for a member of her family? Or maybe she thought the girl was dead. Whatever it was, Ariella was glad of it, for the siege had cost her too much also in terms of her people.

"I am honored by your challenge," Ariella replied in the customary fashion, "But I would like to add one condition. The people within the castle should be free to decide whether to stay or go, no matter the outcome. They may leave and take their livestock and property with them."

"Whither would they go?" Ancarette asked.

"Wherever they like. The important thing is, they were never your subjects, and they never will be."

"Bold words for someone besieged and surrounded on all sides," Ancarette remarked.

"Nevertheless," Ariella replied, "I have spoken them. And another thing, I have your niece. She will be released to you if you agree to my terms."

"That stupid girl!" Ancarette cried. "Keep her for all I care. This is not about exchange of hostages but single combat."

"Then there will be no single combat," Ariella said. She pulled on Destiny's reign to turn the horse back to her castle, but she was only making a show of leaving. Single combat was the way to prevent any more bloodshed.

"What's the matter, afraid you'll lose?" Ancarette taunted.

"Not really," Ariella smirked. She was not lying. Although Ancarette had more experience, Ariella felt she was ready to face her. "Let it be your way. The people stay with the castle, but my warriors will be free to choose their new baroness... no matter the outcome of our combat."

"That's hardly 'my way'," Ancarette scoffed. "But I will agree to this term, especially if you return my niece today. Is there anything else you desire?"

"There is," Ariella said.

"Well?"

She found it hard to say these words, leaving herself vulnerable to Ancarette's mockery. It was almost akin to begging, but she had no choice.

"As you've remarked, this is a small barony," Ariella began, "and I know every single person in it. They are like my family. If I am defeated, promise me that you will not rule over them harshly, that they will not be subjected to hard labor, that families will not be separated, and that they can all continue to live in peace as they had always done."

Ancarette paused, considering this. She seemed to enjoy taking her time.

At last, she nodded.

"This is a fair request, and I will abide by it."

Ariella could not believe her negotiation had gone so well. She had pushed Ancarette to the limit and still secured her warriors their well-deserved freedom, maybe even a chance for the rest of her people to live in safety.

"Tomorrow at noon, then," Ancarette said.

They shook hands. Ariella had never accepted a serious challenge like this before. It was odd, shaking hands with someone and looking into their eyes, those green, dancing eyes of Ancarette, who might be her killer tomorrow. Neither of them said it, but the battle would surely be to the death.

The people stood respectfully at a distance as she rode back. No one dared ask what had transpired between the two leaders. Ariella did not feel ready to announce what had happened. As she dismounted, Jaquelle approached her. The old nursemaid looked exhausted from a sleepless night of tending the wounded. Her hair was escaping from the handkerchief she had tied around her head, and the circles under her eyes looked red and inflamed.

"I agreed to single combat," Ariella said softly, "It is time to end this."

"Good," Jaquelle replied.

Ariella knew that Jaquelle would tell the others, and that soon the news would spread throughout the castle. She went up to her chambers for some much needed rest.

She always slept remarkably well before a battle. She knew that sleep was essential, and there was no use in worrying: the gods would decide her fate upon the morrow.

It had not always been easy for her to accept, but she tried to persuade herself that if the gods had decided to extinguish her family line, if tomorrow was to be her last day on this earth, then there was some reason why it would be for the best. Sometimes, life seemed too hard, and death would perhaps be a relief.

Her only regret was not saying goodbye to Demetrius, but that was also for the best. He belonged to another, and it was no use trying to pretend otherwise. However, there was one thing she could do.

The little glider squeaked when she entered her room. It flew from one piece of furniture to another with a few beats of its wings.

"At last, I have a job for you," Ariella said.

She sat down and wrote the letter. This time, the words came so easily.

My dear D,

Tomorrow I fight in single combat. I may be dead when you read this, but please know that while I live, I love you. It was hard for me to admit that I needed your help, perhaps I still do.

Love,

A

The glider chittered excitedly as she tied the note to its leg. She went up to the roof and released the little creature, knowing that on this moonless night no one would see him fly from the castle and off to Sylcadia.

CHAPTER 15

It was not the worst day to fight, Ariella thought as she rode away from the castle walls to face her opponent. The sun shone through wispy clouds, and the constantly falling snowflakes melted when they reached the yellow dead grass on the ground. And yet, she could feel the tension in the air.

No one said anything as the two parties dismounted and walked towards each other. Ariella took off her red cloak, letting it float to the ground, and Ancarette followed suit.

It seemed Ancarette's people had prepared everything. A patch of barren earth was to be their duelling ground. The firewood doused with oil, which was to be lit around the fighters, was already laid out neatly in a circle of about twenty feet in diameter.

Ancarette's second was a huge man who looked fierce and bear-like in his black fur cloak. Ariella had brought Jaquelle.

"After you," said Ancarette's second.

They all stepped inside the circle. As soon as they did so, he struck a flint and lit the firewood. The circle flared up around them.

Behind the circle of fire, a much larger circle of people was beginning to form. Warriors from both sides had laid aside their arms, and the people from the castle had come down to see their fate being decided. Ariella was grateful for the ring of fire which separated her from the spectators. She already knew well enough what was at stake, and she felt the pressure mount as more and more people arrived to see her fight.

As always, Ariella had her two-handed sword, while Ancarette swaggered forth with a shorter sword and a small shield on her left arm. Both fighters were not wearing helmets and only light armor, chain mail for the body and leather for the arms and legs. Their hair was braided and pinned up to avoid getting singed by the fire or grabbed by an opponent. Ancarette's wild curls looked ready to break free of their confines, but her face did not have its usual complacent and disdainfully mocking look. For the first time, Ariella saw another side of her, a resolute and serious one.

Jaquelle and Ancarette's lieutenant both drew their swords and brought the points together to form a barrier between the two fighters. Then they raised their blades and stepped back, commanding, "Begin!"

Ariella had often seen fighters who would stalk their opponent carefully, making small provocations and trying to judge their reaction and learn their technique. This had never been her way. Especially not now, when she needed to begin and end this duel decisively. If she was going to attack, she would do so with true intent.

As soon as the signal was given, Ariella launched forward, but she was met with brutal resistance. Ancarette was not giving an inch of ground, and she parried each one of Ariella's thrusts and cuts and riposted each time or punched with her shield. Ariella had to defend herself just as forcefully as she was attacking. Each tiny advantage that she gained was quickly taken away. Every time she knew that Ancarette was the tiniest bit unbalanced or off guard, there was no chance to take advantage of it, for Ancarette contrived a way to strike at her and force her back.

The outside world ceased to exist, everything except Ancarette's whirling sword and bludgeoning shield. Ariella had already been struck twice by the metal boss in the center of the shield, but she barely felt the pain, though she knew her arm and ribs would be bruised later. There was no time for anything except anticipating the next assault. Suddenly, she realized she was retreating. Ancarette was pushing her back. Furious, Ariella struck with sudden vigour. Ancarette had not expected it, and the usually graceful baroness leapt back awkwardly. Still, it had not been enough to save her. Ancarette took a few more steps back, clutching her left shoulder.

Ariella knew her sword had cut through the armor. She held her breath, wondering whether the cut she had made would mean victory. Then, she breathed again, disappointed. Ancarette grinned and resumed her guard. It was only a scratch.

"Is this the best you can do?" Ancarette asked in her usual derisive style.

Ariella merely laughed at this taunt. But in the next few seconds her confidence suddenly took a downward turn.

Ancarette was forcing her back much too quickly, until suddenly she felt the heat of the fire. It was too close. The flames burned high, but aside from the danger of being burned, if she stepped or fell into them, she would lose the battle.

Ariella rallied once more, dancing around her opponent to avoid the flames behind her.

They clashed again in the middle of the circle, watched intently by the two seconds, who were constantly on the move to avoid their blades.

Both opponents were still bent on attacking, and neither wanted to cede ground even for an instant. Somehow they ended up simply pushing at each other, swords crossed between them.

Fearing that Ancarette would use the oldest trick in the book, yielding to unbalance her, Ariella wanted to beat her to it, and leapt back. But Ancarette was quick on her feet, and she too sprang away as soon as Ariella did. They stood a few feet apart, catching their breath.

In that moment Ariella realized that even with her nascent Zaliati power, Ancarette was at least her equal in strength and speed. But she did have a weakness, and Ariella formed a new strategy during those few seconds that they stood breathing and glaring at each other.

She had noticed that Ancarette favoured overhead attacks that were flamboyant and powerful but time-consuming. If she were to attempt another one, it would be the perfect opportunity to slash at the exposed right side of her body underneath her arm.

Ancarette charged her again, and their swords clashed. Ariella sensed that this would be the final bout. She was not really thinking, only reacting to each new movement of Ancarette's sword, watching her shoulders and her arms.

At last, Ancarette raised her sword high over her head... Ariella went for the final stroke.

But Ancarette was faster. She had sidestepped and thrust her blade directly forward at Ariella's chest.

At first, Ariella felt nothing. She only cursed herself for being too slow and for letting Ancarette trick her. The flames crackled around her, the faces of the spectators watched her intently, the castle stood lonely upon the hill. She didn't know how bad the wound was.

She saw the answer in Ancarette's eyes. There was elation in those green orbs.

Ariella retreated a couple of steps, trying to give herself room, but suddenly her knees were weak with shock. She fell, dropping her sword.

Then the agony struck.

Panicked, she scrambled to clutch her sword again... it had not fallen very far. She clasped the hilt, but the pain in the right side of her chest was unbearable. She panted, bracing herself for when Ancarette would approach to finish her off.

If she lay still, the hurt was not so great. But she knew she would make one last effort now as Ancarette approached her for the final, mortal blow. Ariella would not let herself be killed like this.

But Ancarette did not approach. Jaquelle now stood between her and Ariella, blocking her way.

"You don't have to kill her," Jaquelle said.

"I told her when this first began, I would spare no one who rebelled against the queen," Ancarette objected. "Now move aside."

"You've already defeated her," Jaquelle pleaded, "do not kill a fellow baroness simply to assuage your anger. It is not done in Dezearre."

"And why shouldn't I? Her foolish rebellion cost me many warriors. Her head will be a fine trophy, and an example to others."

Ariella wished Jaquelle would step aside and not beg for her life. Humiliation even more painful than the wound burned her face. She tried to gather her last vestiges of strength for Ancarette's inevitable attack. She wanted to call out to Jaquelle, but her voice too weak, she did not have the breath.

"The treachery of which she is accused is a false charge," Jaquelle argued. "The truth will emerge sooner or later, and you will regret killing her."

"Step aside, woman," Ancarette ordered impatiently.

Ariella strained her neck to see what was happening. She heard the clash of steel, and by the time she realized what she was looking at, it was all over.

It was not Ancarette herself, but her lieutenant who had attacked Jaquelle, and now his body in its black fur cloak lay on the ground, and she could hear his groans of pain. Two of Ancarette's men pushed the fiery branches aside and hurried over to remove him from the circle.

Ancarette spoke very softly in the ensuing silence. "Now you have truly angered me."

Jaquelle stood firmly between her and Ariella.

"Jaquelle, stop," Ariella cried hoarsely. "I have lost."

"Listen to your baroness," Ancarette said, "I will cut you down."

"Do not challenge me," Jaquelle replied, a definite note of anger emerging in her deep voice.

"Oh, I will not," Ancarette said. "My warriors will capture you, for you are breaking the rules of this combat. Seize her!"

Ariella groaned with anguish. She closed her eyes, unable to witness the scene. She could not bear it that Jaquelle was to be captured because of her.

"No!" a man's voice rang out over the plain.

Ariella did not dare open her eyes yet, but she thought she recognized the voice. But that was impossible. Demetrius couldn't be here.

When she dared to look, she saw Ancarette's warriors hurriedly pushing aside the firewood with their swords and swarming into the dueling ground. Meanwhile, on the opposite side of the circle, another company of warriors leapt over the flames. It was Demetrius, leading several Sylcadian fighters. They were mostly men, for women fighters were more rare outside of Dezearre. They wore long blue cloaks over chain mail, and Demetrius was amazingly majestic, as she had never seen him before.

He gave Ariella only a brief glance, focusing on Ancarette and her followers. The two war bands stood facing each other.

"Where in the Blessed Realms did you all come from?" Ancarette asked. "Who are you?"

Demetrius took a step towards her and bowed respectfully.

"I am Prince Lennell Demetrius of Sylcadia. The baroness of Leduryon is my ally, and I will protect her."

"I bested her in fair combat, prince," Ancarette said. "You have no right to intervene."

"Nevertheless, I will," Demetrius stated. His Sylcadians had already formed a protective circle around Ariella and Jaquelle. "If you wish to kill her, you will have to go through me."

"I don't understand!" Ancarette shouted, "What is it to you? Why did you come all this way just to stop me from taking what's rightfully mine?"

"The castle is yours," Jaquelle stepped in, "you have won it. But I will defend the baroness to the death."

Ancarette glared in turn at Jaquelle and Demetrius. She seemed to be weighing her chances against them.

"You're lucky to be a royal brat, otherwise I would skewer you," Ancarette pronounced disdainfully. "But I have no desire to start a war or to have the king of Sylcadia become my blood enemy. Take this useless carcass if you wish."

Demetrius did not wait a moment longer but rushed over to Ariella and lifted her off the ground. Despite the physical and moral suffering wracking her body, Ariella suddenly felt an upsurge of happiness to be in his arms once again. But when she looked up at his face, she was horrified at the intense look of anger on his features. She had never Demetrius like that before. He kept his eyes forward, not even looking at her.

For a moment, she was afraid to speak to him.

"Let us be off," he said to his people.

"Where are you taking the baroness?" Ariella heard Emelote, the new leader of her guards accost him.

"To a place where she can safely recover," Demetrius replied without stopping or slowing down.

"Then we shall follow," said the guardswoman.

Ariella could not express her gratitude. She was not sure whether her guards would wish to follow her now that she was a baroness without a castle and would probably be dead soon anyway. She felt strangely absent from her own body, even though she could still feel the warmth of her own blood seeping through her clothes.

She was gently handed her over to someone else, a Sylcadian warrior with long grey hair. Meanwhile Jaquelle came over with Ariella's red cloak and wrapped her in it like a blanket. Then Demetrius mounted his horse, and Ariella was passed up into his arms once again.

He wrapped the wings of his cloak over hers for extra warmth.

The horse's roan mane flapped rhythmically as they moved off at a smooth gait.

"You gave up riding Mock?" she asked, hating the sound of her own voice, a mere croak.

For the first time, Demetrius turned to her, something that looked like relief lighting up his face. His lips curved into a faint smile.

"Mock is well taken care of in my stables," he replied, "I

will forever be grateful to him. But for this journey, a slightly faster horse was needed."

Ariella wondered if she was dying, but without much angst. She was willing to accept whatever fate had in store, and to die in the arms of her love would not be the worst way to go.

CHAPTER 16

Ariella awoke, and the snowflakes were still falling.

She was still wrapped up in Demetrius' cloak, cradled in his strong arms, her head resting on his shoulder. Realizing that she was still alive came not as a relief exactly but as a kind of challenge, a challenge she accepted.

So, fate had seen her through, but not without a harsh test. Well, if her fate had not been too kind to her, she would not be too gentle to it either. Instead of following where her fate led, she would now take command. She would fight not only for her existence but also for much more than that. She would fight for him.

The horse hooves sounded lonely on the vast plain. Demetrius was still looking ahead with a troubled gaze.

"Where are we going?" she asked.

He was startled to see her awake again, and now he looked at her, concern furrowing his forehead.

"To a place where you'll be safe," he replied, "Soon we'll find shelter for the night. Jaquelle will tend to your wound. Just hold on, my love. You're not thinking of dying, are you?"

She shook her head.

"Good, that's what I thought," he tried to smile, but his face was too tense.

"Thank you..." she whispered.

Oblivion washed over her once again.

When she awoke next, she was in a bed, and a few rays of morning sunlight were stealing into the room. It was a small room, humble but decorated with a few rugs and simple wooden carvings of animals. A very old woman sat by the bedside. It took Ariella a while to place her, but then she remembered.

"Magdelne?"

"Yes, baroness," the woman replied.

Ariella tried to look down at her wound, and the movement hurt, but not nearly as much as it had before. There was a clean bandage tied just above her breasts, and she was wearing a fresh shirt.

Magdelne held a cup of water to Ariella's lips, and she drank zestfully. She had never derived so much pleasure from a simple glass of water. Then she lay back on the pillow, exhausted by the effort.

"I'm back in your home?" Ariella asked.

"I'm afraid so. You have journeyed far, only to end up back here. But my humble house is yours once again."

"May the god of travelers repay you for your hospitality," Ariella smiled.

"And what's more, your nursemaid cleaned and sewed up your wound, and I think you'll live," Magdelne informed her with that mischievous twinkle in her eye.

Ariella sighed. She had accepted the challenge of living again, but she was not yet sure what she was living for. Her home was lost, and she had to make sure her people had a means of surviving. That was a start.

The old woman took her hand gently. It felt good to the touch, the age-worn skin so delicate, like a flower petal. "How do you feel?"

"Better than yesterday," Ariella pronounced.

"Prince Demetrius is out making ready to leave," Magdelne continued, "so I won't be able to offer my hospitality for long. He sat here with you most of the night, you know."

"He's leaving?" Ariella asked, immediately regretting the

question, for it sounded foolish. Of course he had to be on his way. He had already risked his life for her in the ring of fire. He had saved her, and now he needed to get back to his kingdom.

"Everyone is leaving," the old woman confirmed.

"Magdelne, the last time we were here... why did you ask us when we were getting married?"

The old woman looked out the small window, somewhere out into the fields, then she met Ariella's eyes. "Because," she replied, "I could see that you loved each other. And I can see that he's a good man. He wants to marry you. Baroness, you're hurting my hand..."

"I'm sorry," Ariella said. She released Magdelne's slender, wrinkled fingers, forming her own hand into a fist. "I wish that were true, but it can never be."

She could not believe she had just confided her heart's desire to a woman who was nearly a stranger, but it felt good to do so. Magdelne understood her. Besides, she had kept this love secret for far too long.

"Don't be sad, my dear, the worst is behind you," Magdelne coaxed. "I will bring you some soup, all right?"

Ariella agreed, and Magdelne shuffled out of the room, just as Demetrius appeared in the doorway. It must have been true about him sitting up all night with her. He looked pale and exhausted, though still amazingly handsome in his bright blue cloak.

Ariella could not bear to look at him.

"Demetrius, I'm sorry," she said, lowering her eyes.

"Why ever would you be sorry?" he asked, coming closer to the bed.

"You must hate me for dragging you into this," she replied.

"I wanted to be dragged into this," he assured her. "And I could never hate you."

He sat down on the edge of the bed and looked searchingly into her eyes.

"But you looked so angry..." she began.

"Ariella," he sighed, "I was angry at myself for not having

come sooner. When I saw you lying there, covered in blood, I nearly lost my mind. I thought you were dead. I was afraid to look at you, fearing it might be too late."

"But why are you here?" Ariella wondered.

"Would I abandon my former traveling companion?" he asked gently, "the one who helped me escape from the Chaldeans, who saw me through the dangers of the elf forest, who acted with such talent in Vidor's timeless masterpiece Baconius, Prince of Roanland?"

She smiled faintly. "I mean how did you get here just one day after I replied to your letter?"

"Ariella, I could not rest until I knew you were safe. Two days after I had sent the glider, I was moping around the palace, and I realized that if anything happened to you, I would never forgive myself. I had the persistent feeling that you were in danger. My parents thought I was mad, though that is not unusual in and of itself."

Ariella chuckled despite the pain in her chest. She had missed the way he made her laugh...

"And so I rode to Dezearre. The night before your combat, I was already close to your domain when the glider landed on my shoulder. I read your message, and I rode through the night as fast as I could with my warriors... Well, you know the rest."

"You saved me," she said. "Only so we could go our separate ways again."

"No, Ariella," he replied, leaning towards her, "Why would you think that? Why would I abandon you now? No, you and all your people will be traveling with me to Sylcadia."

Ariella could barely breathe. She tried to sit up, and he helped her, holding her head with gentle care, propping the pillow up so she could lean back on it. A moment ago she had been forlorn at the thought of saying goodbye to him again, but now her heart was racing, elation and terror fighting for space within her injured body.

"But what about..." she began.

"I know," he said, "I know, I am still engaged."

He took her hand, unbending her fingers from the fist she had been squeezing, and kissed it.

"There must be a way for us to be together," he said with determination. "We will find a way. Do you not trust the promise of the crown prince?"

"The crown prince, no," she said. "But that fellow who traveled with me on that long journey, I like him, and trust him."

She truly had her doubts about whether those two people were the same. He had been answerable only to himself during their journey, but now the responsibility of an entire kingdom would rest on his shoulders.

"Magdelne said that you're a good man, that you want to marry me…" she whispered. She could not believe herself, divulging her deepest feelings like this again. But maybe, she decided it was not weakness that made her do it. It was simply wanting everything to be out in the open.

"We both know old Magdelne is never wrong," Demetrius pronounced, his roguish smile irresistible. "What say you, will you come with me?"

There were many reasons not to go, but Ariella could not think about them now. Now that he was here, she would not be able to bear it if he went back to Sylcadia without her. Besides, her people would be safe there, provided for, at least for a while until she regained her strength and thought of a new plan.

"I will," she replied.

Demetrius smiled again, this time in that open, vulnerable way he had in rare moments. He kissed her lips tenderly, giving warmth to her whole body, and for the first time in many weeks, she felt happy to be alive.

The day was cold and misty, but Ariella was wrapped snugly in her red cloak. Over it, warm blankets swathed her whole body. She was traveling in a cart filled with soft hay, and somewhere up ahead, the Sylcadians were riding. Demetrius on his roan horse rode beside her. Jaquelle and her people were walking behind the cart in the tail of the procession, and they were singing.

It was a song whose words were too ancient to be understood, but in the melody she sensed a restless, almost joyous lilt that sounded like hope.

Looking up at Demetrius, she mused that it was appropriate to be seeing him from this angle, for he was far above her station. Of course, she was of noble blood too, but her lineage was not as high as that of a crown prince, unless one counted the lineage of old forgotten heroes. And yet, if nothing else, he was still her friend. He had come for her and saved her. Then why was the pain in her chest so overwhelming? It was more than just the wound. There was a crushing weight that would not go away and a feeling of foreboding. She could sense that nothing would be easy when she arrived in Sylcadia.

But she had made her choice. It was a gauntlet thrown in the face of destiny. She wanted to live, but not merely to exist as she had done before. She believed in her star now. Since life had been given back to her, she was determined to be with Demetrius, to take back her castle, and to avenge the wrongs done by Theodos and Esclairmonde. None of these would be easy to accomplish, but while she lived, she would never stop fighting.

OTHER TITLES BY CAROLEE CROFT

Engaged to the Earl

At twenty one, Martha Darrington was hoping that she still had several years of carefree cavorting ahead of her. She thinks that her time in Bath is only a restful holiday. However, she is shocked to find that her strict aunt has arranged her engagement to the Earl of Bradfield.

Edward would like nothing more but to continue his affair with the possessive Elizabeth Camplyon, while entering into a loveless marriage of convenience with Martha. Seeing that her future husband is not attracted to her, Martha turns to her steadfastly loyal servant Tom for affection. When her wedding is imminent, she tries to win the earl's love using a magic potion, but the plan backfires... in a most sexy way.

Ariella's Rebellion: Book Two in the Stars at Zenith Trilogy

Ariella recovers from her wound and Demetrius tries to make her feel welcome in Sylcadia although his mother and his fiancée, Duchess Edoline make sure that she doesn't.

But while Demetrius is in danger from struggling with his own demons, Ariella knows she can save him, even if it means risking the queen's wrath and never seeing him again.

ABOUT THE AUTHOR

Carolee Croft enjoys traveling around the world, trying chocolate in all its various forms, and relaxing with a good book. She is obsessed with Italian greyhounds.

Connect with Carolee online:

http://caroleecroft.wordpress.com
@CaroleeCroft
http://www.facebook.com/caroleecroft/